THE RIGHTEOUS BROTHER

Adrian Wilson

SPRINGBOARD FICTION

Published by **Springboard Fiction,** School Lane,
Glasshoughton, Castleford, WF10 4QH
tel: 01977 550401/603028
fax: 01977 512819
e-mail: BOOKS@ARTCIRCUS.DEMON.CO.UK

© text: Adrian Wilson, 1997
© cover image: Paul Miller, ergo design
editor: Mark Illis
cover design: ergo design
typesetting: Reini Schühle, Adrian Wilson
                          (Art Circus Education)
production: Reini Schühle, Ian Daley, Clare Conlon
printing: FM Repro, Roberttown, Liversedge

ISBN: 1 901927 00 8
classification: fiction

Springboard is the fiction imprint of Yorkshire Art Circus. We are a
unique book publisher. We work to increase access to writing and
publishing and to develop new models of practice for arts in the
community.
Please write to us for details of our full programme of workshops and
our current book list.
Look in on our Website on: http://www.artcircus.demon.co.uk

Yorkshire Art Circus is a registered charity No 1007443.

Yorkshire Art Circus is supported by:

For two Jacks

Adrian Wilson is a journalist from Wakefield.
This is his first novel.

With thanks to Mark, Lindsay,
Ian, Reini and all at Yorkshire Art Circus.

One

Your first fumbled sex, remember that? Lips that go bump in the night. Fingertips and hot-cold rippled moons of skin. Thumbs and hooks.

The first song that stirred some symphony inside you. The first book you read breathlessly, which spun you with torch under blanket into the small hours to its conclusion. The first exotic dish that made you aware of your tastebuds. Your first car, first job, first alcoholic haze, first marriage, first child, first murder.

Childhood hangs on a web of nonsensical songs. We dangle on strings to nursery rhymes which have their origins in plagues and massacres, war and famine. Something as essentially upbeat, as innocent and modern as *Happy Birthday* can, through its repetitiveness and the unpredictable contours of melody and association, become sinister and ripe with unpleasant connotations, whilst the palsied resignation of *Ring A Ring O' Roses*, or the forgotten screams behind the skipping bars of the big ship sailing up the alley, alley-o, can resonate with all the joy of a bursting heart.

But the song which I hear now, fighting its way from a distant radio through the clatter of leather boots on metal steps, keening above the perpetual badinage which resounds around the corridors and the slamming of heavy doors, is *A Lover's Concerto*, by a group called The Toys. A melody by Wolfgang Amadeus Mozart, to whom such beautiful trifles were an extension of breathing. The song's treatment is second-hand and throwaway, in imitation of the artists on the Tamla Motown label, or Phil Spector's girl groups, perhaps. The words, in as much as I have ever understood them, are cloyingly sentimental, but the combination of these things is irresistible. At five or six years old, oblivious as I was to the emotions the song was expressing, I think it delivered to me an accurate premonition of what a broken heart would feel like.

Do they ever consider that, these Toys, who will now be locked into blue-rinsed and golf-slacked routines?

As for the books, they progressively took me, along with the rest of us children, in search of golden doubloons on desert islands, to the tops of magical trees, to ice caps where all was in twilight hibernation, through old wardrobes, under wire fences and down rabbit holes into parallel kingdoms, to the centre of the earth and out the other side, which was a much darker place. I devoured the future worlds of teenage science fiction full of infinite martial variation and elaborate weaponry, exotic costume, black holes and universal avarice. Until I'd faced enough of possible futures, of travelling through time and space, and I simply stopped reading anything that wasn't required by my studies, or later, my profession.

Firsts, the first things, they were in a dark bottle and its contents were impossible to guess at, until suddenly it was empty. It's the same for everyone.

And then I think of all the other sex, the other music and books, the meals and alcohol and cars and panoramas which, however different they were, were somehow more of the same, only not as good. After the first, it will always be necessary to regret what comes next.

So it doesn't surprise me that I'm here in this cell, with a glue of lemon urinal cubes and cooking fat constantly at the back of my throat, my soft body growing scales under the sheet of scrapings that constitutes a standard issue blanket.

What does surprise me is why I'm here. For putting my signature in the wrong place, it seems, and failing to read between the lines. For an inability to focus on spidery documents drawn up by myopic clerks and for gravely misplacing my trust. Negligence in short, although despite my formal training I am unable to locate just where exactly disinterest dissolved and a cast-iron Duty of Care emerged. Since I am not blessed with the most reliable of memories, I spent perhaps more time than the average greenhorn reciting my Tort cases until they were word-perfect. I grappled with the intricacies of Contract and Shipping, built parallel corridors in my mind labelled *Criminal* and *Common*, but nothing explains my present predicament.

I have my books and the television, and no bills to worry about in here. Since I am an obvious symbol of resentment, due to a combination of my former profession as a representative of the Crown Prosecution Service, and my infamy, they keep me safe from contamination, from block-headed amorousness and general spite. Occasionally they'll bring me something worth eating. Chicken perhaps, or a piece of fish, albeit having the sweet texture and sour aroma of over-boiled roots. But I'm alone, of course, with only my thoughts for company. They won't let me mix, under the circumstances, for my own safety. But what of my sanity? Being safe ceases to have significance.

It's something the psychoanalysts, the reformers and therapists, fail to take into consideration, something so simple my son James understood it instinctively as a baby. He didn't care who was staring into his cot and at what hour. He smiled despite the fearsomeness of the ancient death-masks that were wont to loom above him; despite the nicotine clouds, the whisky vapours, the murderous moods. He smiled for the contact. He'll be three now - unbelievably things have taken almost a year to get to this stage, which is not very far at all - with a couple of septuagenarians supplying the essential contact.

I always imagined that, should my liberty ever be taken away from me, I would simply kill myself. Perhaps, back then, it was conceivable. Not, I hasten to add, because I considered myself a free spirit, nor a particularly courageous one, but because it was something I had often, in fits of professional pique, had cause to consider.

Sometimes, in the middle of some interminable case, between bouts of lachrymose mitigation, ponderous pleadings and the anti-climactic outcome, I pictured myself dangling from a makeshift noose of bed-sheets, a solitary bulb throwing shadows across my contorted features, or lying with wrists wide and eyes scarlet beside the trough of a tiled shower cubicle.

In trying to imagine my freedom suddenly curtailed, I found myself mainly lacking a necessary indifference towards time. Traffic jams gave me anxiety attacks, made my palms tingle and my scalp itch. Bank queues could move me to the brink of tears. Post offices and bus queues conjured up palpitating visions of rationing, of Victorian soup kitchens, poorhouses and penny lines, crushed carriages and clamouring crowds. Only in the premium-rated, cosy confines of the courtroom could I accept the inevitability of ennui. For the rest of the time I was chasing the next, which - I can see now - was an attempted return to the first.

My name is James Hartley Turner and the events of the date of my birth, November 17th 1957, are outlined on a novelty certificate which has somehow conspired to stay with me. I use it folded twice, lengthwise, as a bookmark. It will tell you I share the birthday with Donny Osmond, Steve Davis, Princess Caroline and Eric Bristow, and that we all rolled screaming into this world when the population was just over 51 million and Harold MacMillan was our prime-minister. Back then petrol was four shillings and two old pence a gallon, *Love Letters in the Sand* floated from a thousand radios and Benny Hill leered and scuttled across the screen in our living rooms for the very first time.

The certificate used to hang from the cistern in the toilet of the house I occupied when married and respectable, a room with dimensions to which I have since become accustomed. My relatively happy domestic life over a number of years was chronicled there in the snapshots haphazardly arranged behind a frame on the wall directly opposite the avocado throne. There was a crack along the bottom of the frame's glass and some of the photos had slipped - a clear symbol of the turbulence and disorder which was to follow.

Moving your eyes from the top left hand corner you would have observed a group standing outside a barn in hacking jackets and stout shoes. Next to it was a picture of a man with a rifle over his shoulder and after that the group again, eating sandwiches from Tupperware boxes on a shingle beach.

From these it might reasonably be assumed that the circles I moved in were country-loving and casually prosperous, well-heeled outdoor types, accomplished equestrians; upholders of the status quo.

Next, I'm sure, was a picture of a baby holding a red duck; my son, also called James (which would suggest to you either vanity on my part or, more obviously, adherence to certain family traditions).

James Junior appeared quite often: plastered to the cabin of a yacht in a sou'wester, in dungarees on an expansive sofa, asleep on my wife's shoulder and buried deep in the over-generous crenellations of his top-of-the-range pram, gazed at by adoring grandparents.

Moving quickly on: a trim woman in a grey trouser suit and pearls holds up a camera outside a church, a man in steel-rimmed glasses adjusts a carnation in his lapel, a girl in a large sun-hat extends a beckoning finger to the camera whilst clutching a bottle of *Perrier*. These were minor players really, family and old friends.

Having successfully identified her, you'd probably notice that my poor wife seemingly could not be photographed with her eyes open. She had a rare talent for blinking in perfect synchronicity with the click of a shutter. Her flaxen hair was permanently dishevelled and film conspired to capture her premature double-chin from an unflattering angle. There was something slightly frumpy about her, something straight-laced. If I were to be honest about it, she looked at her most vampish - peaked in the femme fatale stakes - when she started wearing maternity dresses.

Sally - Sal - left two days after it all started, taking James Junior to stay with the woman with the camera, her mother. Because of Kevin, I suppose.

I also had my eyes closed in one of the photographs - a blurred close-up in which I was grinning and grappling with something unseen. The other appearance I made in that flurry of times, places and faces, those snapshots without anchors, was at the kitchen table displaying a trout on a piece of newspaper. Half of a headline was visible at the side of the fish: *New Tax Revolt -*

They were always revolting, the masses, it seemed to me, always willing to complain, object and protest whenever they were called upon to help out in any way, to contribute or chip in. They just wanted too much of everything without personal involvement.

I admit I was perhaps frightened of the seething, bubbling cauldron of avarice and envy which existed largely in my imagination, but such an admission is easy to make now.

Two

I mugged a mugger. That was the first thing.

Ronald Pickles was the name of my assailant, or victim, depending on which way you choose to look at it. It happened right on my own doorstep, as I put the milk bottles out, just before midnight. His intention was - or so I supposed - to quickly overcome me with the element of surprise, springing up from behind a split bag of sand and an overturned wheelbarrow.

Unfortunately I was broader and he failed to push me with enough force against the wall of my home. In his scheme of things I should have conformed to the stereotype, thrown my wallet his way and fallen to the ground in foetal shock. That would have been okay. I was dealing then with someone totally lacking any decent code of ethics or moral consideration for others.

The patio was only half-finished at the time, and looked like a miniature building site. We scuffled in a very undignified way, Ronald and I, the harsh porch lighting stretching our jagged shadows to needle points. There was something half-hearted, something positively uncinematic about our exertions. His damp padded coat cushioned my lips as he tried to wrap his arms around my neck, adolescent stubble chafing my forehead. We parted clumsily and examined each other for a moment, the sparring clouds of our breathing colliding between us. It was all faintly embarrassing. Perhaps that's why neither of us said anything. Violence, when it crops up, should at least allow its participants to believe they are taking part in something tinged with glamour. Glamour justifies everything these days, or at least makes things bearable.

And then he was at me again, bony fingers thrusting for my eyes, lips contorted with unwarranted rage. I gripped his wrists and wrestled him to the ground, feeling the skin of my palms and knees burning against concrete, sand or soil in my hair, on my lips. Blindly I hacked at him with my elbow, crawled away and climbed back up the wall.

I turned to discover that this Ronald Pickles, nose bloodied, was back on his feet and had produced a knife. Finally, in a sentence totally bereft of consonants, he made some kind of demand.

'I beg your pardon?' I said, without really thinking.

With a shiver of restraint he repeated himself, and I got the gist. What I said then by way of a reply will always baffle me. It was certainly cinematic, worthy of Rock Hudson or John Wayne. I now find it hard to believe it was me.

'No,' I told him, 'I have no intention of giving you anything, but I'm going to take everything you have.'

Or words to that effect. What a bastard, eh? I don't doubt for a minute that Ronald is emerging as the hero of this situation. It doesn't surprise me in the slightest.

He gaped at me like a rabbit caught in headlights. There were chip-shop queues in his complexion and his clothing spoke of petty Social Security fraud. It was easy to picture him plying five quid bags of talcum powder outside school gates.

'Drop the knife,' I demanded, calmly. There seemed no need to point out that I was taller and stronger than him and until a couple of years earlier had played regular rugby, or, for that matter, that I thought he had no intention of using his weapon. The knife was almost as pathetic as Ronald himself. It would not have sufficed to skin a rabbit or gut a trout.

Ronald complied of course. The knife clattered to the ground with all the resonance of the tin-foil fish which used to hang above my son's bed, diving for shagpile.

Sally, my wife, cut those fish out and threaded them with cotton, when we were still at that stage of delicious anticipation, awaiting our son, who was swelling in her belly, making her feel like some exotic, over-ripe fruit, and me like some shrivelled seed-spiller. She swelled, I shrank. It's nature.

What was actually taking place between me and Ronald, though it has only now occurred to me, was a form of class war. There was I, privileged, educated, his natural superior, demanding what I knew I was entitled to, namely his respect and obedience. Despite himself Ronald was compelled to bend to my will, to serve me. We were both acting on deeply-instilled instincts, old as society itself.

I should have left it at that, let him scurry away back under his rock, but something made me advance. For a minute I had the strange urge to kiss him. Don't get me wrong, I've never been that way inclined, though I have nothing against those private and consenting adults who are. No, the kiss would have been fitting somehow, a gesture of my forgiveness, compounding Ronald the Serf's humiliation.

It struck me that for too long people like me had been bending over backwards for the likes of Ronald Pickles. We had clothed and fed them, educated them, placed opportunity before them, and when they failed us had nevertheless endeavoured to supply them with basic comforts. They rewarded our kindness with hostility and contempt, wanting nothing less than everything that was ours, and then more. They were waiting for us in the shadows and the litter, their problems filling our papers, straining our budgets and bleeding our resources. Were we, I wondered, many aeons ago, joined by the hip to this subspecies? Was that why we still felt the need to cosset them?

There, amidst sacks of concrete and sand, a jumble of breeze blocks and abandoned tools, I prised my fingers into Ronald's pockets, pulled out first a crumpled five pound note and then a laminated bus pass from which his face stared out sombrely, turned and walked calmly back inside. I waited for a while, before going back out, with the shotgun snaking in front of me, cartridges stuffed in my pockets. For all I knew he could still have been out there, trying to make sense of what had just happened to him, but somehow I doubted it.

For some reason I got it into my mind he'd call the police.

That wasn't as far-fetched as it sounds. Muggers, I am well aware, have rights, as do trespassers and poachers, gypsies and child-molesters. And still the masses make their demands, pressing their revolting blackmail notes into our palms.

The sky seemed unsettled, the wind was furrowing the fields. He'd gone, and I tried to persuade myself then that his presence was just a temporary aberration on my landscape.

13

I went back inside and looked in on Sally and James Junior to find them curled together in contented sleep. As I contemplated my certificate and the photographs in the toilet I was still clutching Ronald's ragged fiver and the bus pass. Butterflies fluttered in my stomach and my breathing was irregular. Without a doubt I had just done something quite uncharacteristic, not to mention preposterous in its implications. It was another first, and even though I didn't acknowledge it at the time, I sensed it had somehow changed things.

Three

The next morning, a Saturday, we were blessed with a visit from Liz Armstrong.

This too, was a first, but after a restless night in which my dreams were full of splintering wood and bunched fists, and the slightest sound from outside was enough to set my heart racing, it was the last thing I needed.

Having kissed Sally on both cheeks in the continental manner and accepted her offer of coffee, Liz pushed her way into the lounge, throwing her briefcase onto the sofa, plugging her lap-top uninvited into a socket to recharge and turning her attention to James Junior.

He was playing with a toy train on the carpet and she pitched off her heels and got down on all fours with him, waddling in her business suit, tights rustling.

Usually we would meet every six months or so, in the lobby of a country hotel, or wedged into a hire car. More often than not she was irritable through running to deadlines and general fatigue, having whirlwinded around the motorway network or perhaps even caught a plane to romance or brow-beat our customers. Wine, dine, flatter and forget. She would peer into the depths of the lap-top as if it were a crystal ball and intersperse fragments of its baffling data with frank details of her amorous liaisons. These involved men with credentials, regardless of their age or virility. Stature was her aphrodisiac, grand titles her titillation. Her padded coffin was my father's old office at the mill and she dipped her fangs into arteries of power and influence. But at the same time she was vulnerable. Running away perhaps from what she was really chasing.

Insecurity in personal relationships, I diagnosed, had provided her with the steely determination necessary to stamp her mark on the world in other ways.

'So this is your beautiful boy. Why do they have to grow up, Turner?'

I took her question as it was intended, as an insult, of course, and a complaint. The women in my life by this time had the knack of inflicting at least a couple of body blows with even the most innocuous of remarks.

Our meetings were always a source of some anxiety, in that I would attempt to cleave my way through her gobbledegook - a mixture of obscure chemical formulae and stockbroker slang - only to be made to feel like a small child asking inappropriately naive questions at every juncture.

But significantly, this was the first time she had actually been to my home.

'What is it James? A choo choo? With a moo cow in the carriage?' she trilled, and then, in a harder tone, addressed me, like a gangster, from the corner of her mouth, 'I'll need you to go through a few things with me this morning. I was at the office until after midnight getting it all in order for you.'

'Don't teach him slang,' I said pointedly. 'It's a train, and a cow. A symbol of everything that's wrong with this country and a potential slab of burger mix respectively. What things?'

'Grumpy old Daddy, isn't he Jimmy-wimmy? Scowly-wowly crabby misery goat. Just your approval for a few recent projects, stock adjustments, some transference of capital involved. Fibre prices are static, but the adhesives are going through the roof. Resins resilient. Binders booming. So that's where we're turning our attention. Speculate to accumulate. Have a look in my briefcase, it's all together in a blue folder.'

·Reluctantly I walked over, flicked the gold-fringed caramel case open and took out the thick file, peering into it without removing anything.

Liz stopped and looked up at me.

'It won't bite you,' she said, before being urged by a shrieking Jimmy-wimmy to resume her hobbled canter.

'Well I'm not going through this lot today,' I said. 'I'll need some time to wade through it all.'

With a groan Liz hauled herself to her feet and pulled James Junior up into her arms, where he busied himself by fondling the row of thin necklaces at her throat and drinking in her *Chanel* in his unashamed, curious manner.

'There's nothing there that directly concerns you,' she said. 'It's all clear enough. I've marked the places where you need to put your signature on each document.'

I shrugged.

'I still need to go through them. I'll find time over the weekend and they can be back on your desk first thing Monday morning.'

I was being deliberately difficult, of course. I didn't really care, but whatever she needed my approval for must have been important, to make a personal visit necessary.

'God, Turner, it's a bit late in the day to be suddenly wanting some hands-on involvement.'

'I hardly have the time for that.'

'Well then.'

'Well then, what?'

'What's wrong, don't you trust the team all of a sudden?'

Sally entered and ignored my exasperated eyebrows as she set down cups and saucers on the coffee table.

'I've heard so much about you, it's nice to meet at last,' she said to Liz, who now had my son on her back and was carrying him in circles around the toy track. 'It must be hard doing what you do. I don't know where you get the energy.'

'It's still very much a man's world Sally, believe me.'

Again, at least a couple of strikes here - a deft swipe at me, a jab to the memory of my father, and perhaps a knee in the groin in the direction of whatever corporate cretin she was currently tailing. She was tired of rolling from silvery barrel-chests, was the implication, weary of whispering sweet nothings to rich nobodies.

'You look well on it, anyway.'

Did I detect dissatisfaction in my wife's voice? Was she trying to imply something, hinting neglect?

'I'm feeling well too, thank you,' Liz replied, 'can we catch the choo choo James? There it goes again. Giddy up! Whoa boy!'

'Are you pleased to see Auntie Liz, James? We'll know where to come for a baby-sitter now, won't we?'

Sally threw me a smile intended to be reassuring and intimate when she said this.

'She's not his auntie,' I quickly pointed out. 'Don't confuse him, Sal. He's never met her before.'

My wife winced and looked away from me. Liz chose to ignore the remark.

'I'd have him any day, wouldn't I my little angel? God, he's gorgeous.'

'As long as you could give him back again after a few hours, eh?' Sally said to Liz.

'I suppose so,' was the reply, framed by a tone of sadness.

Sally coloured when she realised it was possibly the wrong thing to say, when for all she knew Liz may have craved children of her own. But the men Liz wanted already had them, just as they had most other things.

'That's a lovely suit, by the way,' my wife added quickly.

Sally was probably feeling a little dowdy without make-up, in her grey tracksuit and battered trainers, her lank hair flattened, devil-horned and calf-licked, clammy from some ghastly work-out in front of the television.

'Thank you,' Liz said, climbing to her feet again. James Junior began throwing himself at her legs in a rapture of physicality, attempting to skittle her over. 'A necessary extravagance, I'm afraid. How about you?'

'Oh you know...'

The two women exchanged an empathetic look.

'I have to go out,' I said, 'this really is a bad time, Liz.'

'Well before you do, I have to have six cheques signed. Today. Minimum. That's if you really can't spare me ten minutes or so. That's all it will take.'

'I've told you, they'll be on your desk, first thing. Nothing can be so urgent, can it?'

Struggling across the carpet with James Junior hanging on her ankles, she produced the company's master cheque book and handed it to me. Two signatures required.

'Why can't Franklin do it?'

Doddery Franklin had been my father's right-hand man and was now a director. In his seventies, he still hung about the mill like an amputee feeling for the ghost of a limb.

'On holiday.'

'Well that's a first.'

'They're for suppliers, that's all. I don't think you realise...' Her mobile phone started ringing and she pulled it out and began to hold a conversation which sounded like an obscure shopping list, encouraging me to sign the cheques with her eyes and turning the pages when I hesitated.

'Matching tambours...polyprop...*Oasis* supers...royal blue, heavy pile...four modular...adjustable backrests...'

With a shrill *Ciao!* she snapped down the truncated antenna.

'I don't mind making the decisions, but when I'm not there a little initiative wouldn't go amiss wouldn't you think? Thank you.' She grabbed the cheque book from me. 'Go through it all if you must, but I need it back Monday.'

At which she turned, and raising her arms like wings swooped down on James Junior, pushing her face down to his, making gurgling noises as her tongue wagged quickly from side to side. In a fit of giggles he lay prone on his back like a puppy.

'What a shame they have to grow up,' Liz repeated.

'You didn't mention having anything on this morning,' Sally said to me, accusingly.

'You go, Turner,' Liz interjected, 'it will be nice for me and Sally to chat. Let's face it, we've known about each other for so long now, it's like we're family.'

Sally beamed at this. 'And of course, I need a bit more time with this cherub...but please let me have those documents on Monday.'

Her talons dived down for the near-hysterical young bundle again.

You'll know Liz, or somebody like her. She was now responsible for my father's mill, and the laboratory attached to it, from which, at least once a month, a cloud of something noxious, something that gagged and brought tears to the eyes, something potentially blinding, cell-clogging, heart-stopping, would erupt, necessitating evacuation of the premises.

White-smocked, my father and Liz had often worked through the night in there, huddled together over bubbling vats, grinding up mysterious substances in caveman bowls, pumping poison through rubber pipes. The results of their endeavours, it seems, were vastly profitable. Treatments, formulas, catalysts.

I suppose it was inevitable that she'd grasp the nettle when he croaked. Plucky Liz. In a way, I was full of admiration for her. Her dedication and resolve made Liz my father's natural business successor, not that he could ever have accepted it.

As a consequence, she looked younger and certainly more attractive than she had years before, layered and moulded in leading salons and exclusive clinics, sculpted in private hospitals and toned up on farms, pampered by personal assistants, championed by couturiers and perhaps even serenaded by a couple of pioneering surgeons.

She was crisp as a freshly-minted note and the colours of her spectrum were somehow brighter and bolder than the mere mortals she moved amongst. Still, for some reason, she exuded all the sadness of a bald Christmas tree in an Easter skip.

I had nowhere to go, but somehow the two women, although meeting for the first time, conveyed to me the idea I was surplus to requirements. Had I stayed, they would have complicitly exerted some kind of unspoken pressure. An instantaneous heart-to-heart was desired by both, I sensed. They were free to talk about me if they wanted, and whatever else they had on their minds. Emotions could be outpoured, bonds of sisterhood sewn. That kind of thing.

Out in the garden I looked for indications of my scuffle the previous evening with Ronald Pickles. A few skids of sand and toppled bricks were all it amounted to. I saw a spade leaning against the wall and wondered why I hadn't picked it up and whacked him with it. For a few minutes I searched for his knife, but couldn't find it. Then I spotted Kevin hovering on the horizon, at the entrance to a small wood haloed by the bright, low sun.

I knew I would have to do something about him shortly.

I started to walk with deliberation towards him, out of the garden and onto a field that was spongy one minute, hard as ice the next, slippery and then syrupy by paces. Kevin saw me and melted into the trees.

Some long lost combination of smells - the turned soil and its frozen patches of moss, charred stubble, now fossilised, and clay, the bite to the air - reminded me of my childhood and the farm on which I was brought up. It was not far from Skipton and York, close to the Moors.

Sometimes, in the school holidays, I'd play with the son of the farmhand, Brian Bennet. The Bennets lived in a tiny cottage on the edge of the estate. Its timber front was visible from the main road, since on it, in whitewash, were daubed the slogans ANIMAL FEED and KINDLING. The smells of woodsmoke and mutton fat, damp and urine emanated from that dark, windowless place. The toilet could reveal nothing about the Bennets since there wasn't one. Even their shit, fertilising his fields, was in service to my father. But you could shout a wish down to the bottom of the well, which Mr Bennet had dug himself, ten yards from the front door. I was seldom officially allowed into their medieval abode, their dark-ages dwelling. They were embarrassed about me. I didn't belong. My father was a constant, unmentioned presence.

Brian's father was hollow-cheeked and taciturn, with a cough like a handful of stones hurled down a marble staircase. He had a rusting motorcycle with a sidecar in which he used to patrol the fields for stray sheep and poachers. Reluctantly, as if my father breathed at his shoulder, he'd let us go with him, kneeling on a coarse blanket in the box with its creosoted, mud-spattered panels and polythene windscreen.

Brian was a carrot top with an engaging smile. Often I had difficulty understanding his thick local burr. He knew where there were birds' nests and rabbit warrens, even a badger set. He caught small fish with improvised lines and was building a den in a nearby wood. I loved being with him - he had a rooted sense of belonging I deeply envied. The outside world rarely intruded on his territory. This, and the fact that my association with him would surely have brought the blood to my father's cheeks, made his company irresistible.

Our friendship was to end one afternoon, over something petty.

I can't even remember what we were doing now, what wild game we were playing. The sun had blazed all morning as we tramped through the cornfields. I think we were both a little light-headed and our friendship had reached one of those intoxicating peaks that can never be sustained. For whatever reason, Brian threw a stone at me, which caught me in the face. He was mortified, thinking he'd blinded me. I can remember the blood pouring into my eye, but the wound turned out to be superficial. Brian took me back to the cottage where his mother insisted I be taken home. Mr Bennet, filled with foreboding, was reluctant to do this, but eventually did.

On the journey back to the house in the suddenly hateful sidecar, full of outraged privilege as my vision reeled, I imagined what would happen. My father would be furious. He would summon them in with a curled finger and make Mr Bennet hold Brian firmly. I would be instructed to beat him with a walking stick. Mr Bennet would cough phlegm onto the lapel of his jacket as he restrained his son, writhing like an eel. I would strike Brian half-heartedly at first, but quickly realise this would not satisfy my father. Brian would cry and swear, but there would be no way out of the situation. Eventually the stick would sail through the air and make contact with the bridge of Brian's nose with a crunch of cartilage, drawing sufficient blood, at which point Mr Bennet would release his son. My father - for whom the Old Testament concept of justice was surely invented - would then seize the stick and begin to beat his employee.

This however, was not what happened at all.

My father did not want to extract vengeance on my behalf. His peculiar show of belittling my trauma, and actually joking with Brian Bennet's father, to whom I had only ever witnessed him uttering curt commands, sent me skittling into the arms of my mother. She eventually cajoled me, breathless with indignation, towards the staircase, but not before I witnessed the bizarre sight of James Montgomery Turner, my fearsome father, taking up Brian Bennet in a bear-hug and raining kisses down on his forehead and cheeks, as Mr Bennet looked on, impassive. Did I remember incorrectly, or were there tears in his eyes?

I was now at the spot where I'd seen Kevin, and a magpie swooped a yard away from me, pecking at a scrap of something shiny before soaring up into the bare boughs. I dipped down to examine a cluster of toadstools, unplugging one and crumbling it between my palms, its texture like the meat of a fantastical creature, stringy and resilient; raw white. I breathed in its pungency, held it to my lips and dabbed it with the tip of my tongue. Turning, I looked for a suitable young conifer I could fell under festive cover of darkness in the coming week. Sally would decorate it with paper chains and pendants of chocolate.

One Christmas in my childhood, the Bennets were invited to dine with us, up at the farm. In making the effort, showing appreciation and extending the hand of friendship in the season of goodwill, we were doing them the ultimate favour. They arrived as if for a Royal Variety Performance, father and son in stiff white shirts and ties under funereal suits reeking of mothballs, wild ginger hair welded to their foreheads with spit. Mrs Bennet, in an elaborate concoction of home-made sequins and lace.

The evening started pleasantly enough, although I was rather surprised when Brian asked to watch the television and was told we didn't have one. I didn't even think they had electricity in that shack they inhabited. On receiving this information, he turned on me with vicious glee. This was, apparently, an immeasurable triumph for him. To the discomfort of his parents he then began pointing out all the other absences - no fridge or electric cooker, record player or toys. After that the conversation and games were stilted and my father played the clarinet for an interminable time, as the rest of us looked at our feet and tapped politely.

At the end of the evening my father led Brian and myself to the Christmas tree and indicated two presents beneath it. One was the size of a cigarette packet, the other much larger. It seemed obvious the bigger gift would be intended for myself, and without hesitation I grabbed it, curtly lobbing the other gift at Brian and ripping the wrapping from my prize. But mine turned out to be a useless one-thousand-piece jigsaw of Buckingham Palace, whilst Brian's was a top-of-the-range Timex watch. The presents were obviously mixed up, but why had my father not marked them? It was clearly some kind of test, and one that I had failed.

My bewilderment gave way to unrestrained tears, and Mr Bennet tentatively suggested that really Brian should give me the watch and he take the cheap puzzle. But my father insisted that I had made my choice and that should be that.

As my tears escalated into a full-scale tantrum, the Bennets gratefully took their leave. Later, as I lay in my bed still choking with betrayal and heartache, I was aware of an argument raging below me, before finally my father left the house, slamming the door behind him.

Ever after, Brian delighted in detailing the high points of the previous night's TV whenever we met, making a point of displaying his Timex.

Lost in dredging up these private things, I had somehow retraced my steps back across the field, oblivious to its erratic surface, still rolling the fungous strands between my fingers. The door to the house jolted me back to the present. I stepped into the hall to raucous laughter from the lounge.

'It's not that they don't enjoy talking,' I heard Sally say, 'just that they don't want to talk about what you want to talk about.'

'Oh, they love to talk,' - Liz - 'especially with alcohol inside them. And self-importance. But listening's a different thing. It's what they're taught. Carry the ball and run with it. Pretend you're playing for the team, but don't pass.'

I turned and fanfared the door against its frame. Abrupt silence, then stifled giggles. I rattled the door to the lounge before entering.

Visibly flushed, Sally was draped on the sofa, with James Junior sleeping contentedly at her breast. With exaggerated slow-motion she was raising a finger in the air and drawing it slowly to her nose, going cross-eyed, which sent Liz - in a complex arrangement of spread-eagled thighs and sprawling elbows down on the carpet - into another fit of giggles. Two empty wine bottles stood amongst the debris on the coffee table.

'It was supposed to go to my lips,' Sally said breathlessly, her head thrown back against a sofa arm.

Liz straggled to her feet.

'Turner,' she slurred, 'we fucking love you. All of you.'

'He's really too old for that now, Sally,' I said formally, gesturing at the goldfish lips of my son against her purple nipple. 'Two years old, for God's sake. Especially in company.'

Liz pushed against me.

'But you never really leave it, do you?' she said, a flattened palm against the top of her rib-cage, under her tit, pushing herself up to me. 'Can you remember what it tastes like Turner?'

Her perfume had combusted with the wine and I could feel the heat coming from her body in a wave.

'You'd better go,' I said, catching her weight as it slumped against me.

Sally writhed an objection, slipped James from her and stumbled to her feet.

'She can't drive now.'

'She'll be all right.'

'You take her home.'

'She'll be fine.'

We waved her goodbye as she fell into the car. Me stiffly, Sally hovering, beetroot-faced.

'Need that stuff Monday,' Liz managed to say as the electric window encased her, before her black Alfa Romeo needled down the drive and out onto the road.

'I like her,' Sally said as we stood at the door, 'she's great fun.' Again, this was not a simple observation. It was judgement, and physical. Provocation. Bunched fists, pointed fingernails. 'I think I'll take James upstairs for an hour.'

She didn't mean me.

Four

It saddens me greatly to think of all the things my son will be forced to go without. Sal's parents will try and overcompensate, of course, spoiling him, pandering to his whims. They have the money to secure a decent education for him and perhaps are already scheming to provide him with a false identity. Papers arrive concerning his welfare which I simply sign without reading. Pointless contesting anything at this late stage.

My own father died over five years ago, and my mother four years before that. He left behind the Wakefield mill, of course, interests in a string of chemical subsidiaries and the proceeds from the sale of the farm - all of which I assumed would inure me forever against having to cut corners or take stock. I was though, it must be said, as negligent in scrutinising the fine detail of the documentation relevant to my inheritance as I am now in that relating to my son.

It wasn't enough, in any case. My father could never compensate me. He made me what I was with all the faults I readily acknowledge. I was unable to give or receive pleasure without a sense of panic. At times I squandered small fortunes in imitation of hedonism, looking for the first. There was too much of him in me. My father despised simple enjoyment. There were no pictures in our house, no radio or TV. Furnishings were functional, the aesthetic shunned. It rubbed off. I suffered at school, through an ignorance of *The Man from U.N.C.L.E.* and *Juke Box Jury*. There were books, but nothing to stimulate the imagination, just unembellished facts to match the plain furniture. I crammed my forming mind with descriptions of internal combustion engines, colonial history and algebraic formulations. I read about the world in the mean-spirited encyclopaedia and atlas that contained no pictures, only diagrams and maps. Occasionally though, my imagination would slip the reins, take adventurous and literary turns, for instance in that period when I was Tom Sawyer to Brian Bennet's Huckleberry Finn.

I look upon my boarding school years with affection now. The rigid regulations, inferior food and lack of privacy were an improvement on my home. I was diligent and hard-working and I had no fear: no gowned master could fill me with terror the way my father could. Being an only child, dormitory life, with its bullying and mob rule, its atmosphere of uncertainty and its myriad nonsensical rituals, involved a form of intimacy I quickly came to depend on. I excelled on the rugby field too, perhaps finding solace in the tangle of bodies, the mud, the exertion and the sweat.

Returning home was a nightmare. My shrunken doll of a mother and dominant shadow of a father inhabited a loveless, monochrome world.

After my father's funeral, driving away alone (Sal refused to attend), I found myself suddenly overcome with laughter. Tears of hysterical relief rolled down my cheeks. It seemed to me then that I would never again be compelled to seek anyone's approval.

It was, I suppose, in seeking that approval that I took my Articles without having any real sense of vocation. I never took Silk though, which of course deprived me of anything more than being damned with faint praise. Often I was made to feel like a bumpkin by Queen's Counsel, who would descend from the cities to defend some legally-aided lout fit only for the municipal dump.

Now of course, I desperately miss the cosiness of the Magistrates' in Wakefield, or over at Wetherby or Pontefract, the shabby pomp and ceremony, the verbal jousting, the winks and jokes with the defence, scalding-hot coffee with clerks and reporters.

I miss too, that sense of being woven into a historical tapestry, of acting in a well-rehearsed costume drama with a nonsensical plot. My role was one of fawning servility tinged with irony - the jester in court if you wish - attempting, on occasions, to introduce a note of levity, to place individual calamities into their wider context. I spent the best part of a decade rising and bowing like an absurd marionette, listing the misdemeanours of the less fortunate, braying for natural justice on behalf of the Crown Prosecution Service and requesting my costs.

Should you sense dissatisfaction in my tone, don't think for a moment that I could have gone to the other side. The temptation to laugh out loud whilst painting some dangerous psychopath whiter than a biological machine wash would have been too great.

Nor could I have adopted the required tone of sincerity whilst attempting to explain in whispers the complex machinations of the court to some piece of pondlife with his Borstal gloves trailing the ground.

I could never have been Colin Chatterton, the liberal, Legal-Aided leech who often sat to my right in the court rooms, mopping up the monosyllables of his clients as he twiddled with the diddicoy band in his earlobe and dusted the cigarillo ash from his denim shirt, smugly brow-beating me and flashing his Bambi eyes at the bemused probation workers. But let's not mention Colin at this moment.

I was, by necessity, blind to the problems of those people from whom I extracted compensation on behalf of the Crown. We occupied the same city, but my security walls and electronic doors, the doormen of my clubs and associations, and the guards and security networks of the official corridors I stalked, denied them admission.

But in struggling with the mugger Ronald Pickles outside my door that night, it was as if I was being sucked down into the world they occupied.

Five

I didn't kill Kevin, but without a shred of evidence, Sally, as judge and jury, returned a unanimous guilty verdict, and she left me because of it - because of him - taking my son with her. Or at least, that's what I thought at the time.

Oh, I possessed the *mens rea* all right - the intention, in layman's terms - and a very specific one at that. Malice aforethought, beyond reasonable doubt as it were. But the *actus reus*, which must in all cases be established, that was someone else's department. And anyway, the case would never have stood up in court.

Kevin really fancied himself, it has to be said. Big-boned and athletic, he had that macho strut off to perfection. Not much between the ears as it turned out, but then not all women go for that do they? Not all the time. He compensated with enthusiasm and energy. I envied him his full head of hair. Unfortunately I was already thinning - another legacy from my father.

He messed things up for himself, did Kev. His future was assured. I would have continued to treat him well. His duties were light and his living quarters more than adequate. Things would have been fine, I thought, between me and Sally, if it hadn't been for him. In the end I couldn't tolerate all that eye contact going on under my very nose, the electrical brushes and strokes, the brushstrokes of sexual frisson I was supposed to turn a blind eye to.

It was upon spotting Kevin's photograph there in the toilet though, tucked into a corner amidst the scenes from our happy life, that perhaps the green-eyed demon slumbering at the pit of my being was finally fully-roused.

Below the selection of James Junior, there was an over-exposed shot of Sally in a green party hat with rouged cheeks and her eyes closed. Her father, the historian, was at her side, wearing a Father Christmas false beard, an elaborately-iced cake in the foreground. Towards the bottom of the frame there were a few snaps from restrained parties, out-of-focus gyrations around a collapsed buffet, pink-eyed clusters; other people's children; the odd square of rugged landscape. But that Saturday evening, as I strained to the rhythms of time and re-read the familiar certificate to remind myself that I shared a birthday with Auberon Waugh, Peter Cook and Rock Hudson, I sensed that this lower sequence had been disturbed, that something was somehow different. It was then, to my disgust, that I discovered an instamatic image of Kevin had crept in there. Some hundred yards or so behind Sal and James making sand castles on the beach at Robin Hood's Bay there he was, in smug half-profile. My betrayer.

I glared at his image and my rage grew as I remembered the day in question. He'd made what should have been a pleasant trip arduous, with his incessant jabbering, his crude demands on Sally's attention and my patience, constantly pushing his gormless head between the seats in order to get closer to her. There had been something altogether brutish about his lack of tact. To compound matters he'd taken the steep steps down to the beach effortlessly, with Sally almost running to stay at his side and yours truly reduced to a cautious and red-faced snail ten paces behind, like an oil sheikh's wife; like an attendant footman. Wise guy. Obviously he'd decided I was a soft touch by that stage.

If further proof is needed of my benevolence, my paternalistic attitude towards him, then surely the fact that I used to allow him along with us on our days out to the coast speaks volumes. I was aware he seldom had the opportunity to get away.

Sally must have slipped the photograph in behind the frame, there could be no other explanation. Had she actually consciously contrived it, I was forced to wonder? Gaining some sick satisfaction from the secret knowledge that the ghostly presence of my rival for her attentions would be perfectly positioned to mock me each morning as I moved my bowels?

Other spirits stared down from the montage: James Montgomery Turner threatened the camera with flinty eyes and puritanical pursed lips as he attended to an immaculate handwritten ledger at his bare desk; inspected a pasty line of factory workers at the mill; turned a page on a music stand with his clarinet in his hand; contrived a thoughtful pose as he blew pipe smoke from the cab of a tractor. Moira, his wife, my mother, in a coat with a huge fur collar, looked already haunted.

Six

I suppose what people know of me would hardly give them reason to believe me a sympathiser with the feminist cause, but I wouldn't like to treat anyone with the lack of respect my father showed my mother. He bullied her into becoming a pathetic shadow of himself, mouthing his stock of dour platitudes and reinforcing his warped moral code. In daydreams I would often represent my mother in her divorce proceedings, something which would of course be entirely unethical, even if I still held my licence.

I'd have had little trouble though, establishing a case of advanced mental and physical cruelty.

'Would you say you were a generous man, Mr Turner?' I'd begin, reasonably enough.

'Answer the question, Mr Turner,' I would also say, having quickly assumed wig, gown and gavel, this being my fantasy.

'I am a good provider.'

The statement is oily with self-satisfaction, a slick of intolerance.

'Is it not true then, that in thirty years of marriage you never once took your wife on holiday?'

'She didn't like holidays.'

'Why was that?'

'I would have loved to go away,' my mother protests from the other side of the court.

'Mrs Turner, please,' I reprimand her kindly, twirling the gavel in my fingertips, 'you're not supposed to say anything at this stage. I realise this must be rather distressing for you.'

I can't get her face in focus. There is no sense to her holes and orbs, her scrolls and matting. For the moment she must remain half-formed, embryonic.

'So you never took her on holiday,' I continue from the prosecution bench, 'yet you say you were a good provider.'

'She never wanted for a thing.'

It's that certainty I want to snap, that unbending self-belief.

'When was the last time you took her out anywhere?'

'I'm a very busy man. Business makes its demands.'

'But can you remember?'

'Not immediately, no.'

My father tries to subdue me with a thunderous stare, his clenched knuckles white and impotent at his sides.

'Sounds to me as if she took very little providing for. She wasn't well, was she, your wife?'

Suddenly there is shocked recognition on my father's face as he realises what direction the questioning is about to take.

'No,' is all he can manage to stammer.

'No, she wasn't well, or no...'

'Objection.'

'Overruled.'

My father's brief really isn't up to the job, lacking, though I hesitate to admit it, the charlatan flair of Colin Chatterton and his ilk - a tame, prematurely-stooped junior with his mind only half on the case. What are you expecting, a fair trial? I thought we'd already established that life is often anything but fair?

'What steps did you take to ensure she got better?'

'I...'

'Didn't you scorn her perpetual shivering as an appeal for sympathy?'

'I......'

'Didn't you ignore the fact that she continually wheezed like a faulty radiator?'

'Never...'

'Would you say then, Mr Turner, that you are an exacting man?'

'I'm not sure what you mean.'

'That you have high standards?'

'Certainly.'

'Indeed. High standards. Yes indeed. Did these high standards,' - the disdain in my voice is pronounced here, I roll my eyes at the jury, rubbing my chin - 'not include such stipulations as the scullery fire always being lit at five in the morning - as you slept on soundly - with four sticks and two pieces of coal measuring no more than three inches by two inches...'

'Objection your honour, this is all surely irrelevant...'

'Overruled.'

'That your breakfast be served at seven precisely, by your pocket watch, and contain two freshly-laid duck eggs boiled for exactly seven minutes, with bread cut into one inch strips, a level teaspoonful of salt in a mound at the side of your plate, tea stirred in its pot at one minute intervals for at least five minutes, to be served concurrently.'

'I really don't see that this...'

'One more unnecessary interruption of the proceedings,' I inform the cowed defence from under my wig, 'will have severe consequences. Please continue Mr Turner.'

'Thank you, your honour. Now where was I? Ah, yes. Let us move to the subject of cleanliness, shall we? Cleanliness, would you not say, Mr Turner, is next to Godliness, is it not?'

My father's head is bowed now. Is he beaten?

'I'm sorry, I don't think the court could hear that.'

He straightens his back, squares up to the jury.

'Cleanliness is next to Godliness,' he booms. There it is again, that iron certainty. I'll have him yet.

'Thank you. So that, once you had eaten your substantial breakfast, been bathed and dressed and tramped off to your business, it was left to your wife to clean. And you were exacting in your expectation of just what clean implied, weren't you? At the risk of boring the court, perhaps I should just elaborate on what exactly 'clean' means, in terms of the expectations of the accused. With your permission, your honour?'

'We're all ears Mr Turner.' I'm beginning to get restless at the bench. This is a case on which I've already passed judgement, my *obiter dicta* stretching to several volumes.

'All clothing worn once, bed linen and curtains to be washed, aired, ironed and back in their allocated place by noon each day. Floors to be scrubbed, walls to be washed and surfaces to be polished by two in the afternoon. Your honour, ladies and gentlemen of the jury, this may not seem such a formidable task to those of us accustomed to automatic washing machines and dryers, to high-powered vacuum cleaners and all manner of time-saving gadgets, but let me stress that this woman's tools were little more than cold water, stiff bristles and the frail, broken machine that was her own body.'

'We take your point, Mr Turner. Is that it?'

'Not quite, your honour. Mr Turner. Sometimes things were not quite to your specifications were they? Sometimes your leisurely inspections would reveal that a freshly laundered bedsheet showed traces of damp, say, or that a crease remained in the cuff of a work shirt.'

My father's head has drooped once again, under the collective gaze of the jury. His brief has his head in his hands.

'So you'd lock her in the reserve larder, wouldn't you?'

There is a gasp from the jury, and I find myself in full flight now.

'The larder that was never cleaned or stocked, that existed solely to collect dust and grime for her to contemplate in the darkness. And afterwards, on these occasions, is it not also true that you would drag her out and hold her head down in a sink full of cold water in front of your son? 'I'll show you clean,' you would rage, 'let's see how clean things can be with a bit of effort!'

I pause now, to let the full horror of my revelations sink in. The judge shows no inclination to break the stunned silence. Finally, almost whispering, I start to sum up.

'Her life with you has been one long nightmare of intimidation and drudgery. You could easily have afforded help in the maintenance of your huge house, but you preferred to leave it all to an unpaid servant. No, not a servant, no servant would have endured such treatment. A slave. She cooked and cleaned, washed your shirts and looked after your son, always terrified that the hands of the clock would move too quickly and you'd return before she was done. There were no holidays for her to look forward to, no nice new clothes for her to step into when she wanted to feel loved, no flowers, no little words of encouragement to chivvy her along...'

My mother can't help getting to her feet again, jubilant and full of adoration for her son.

'Let the old bastard have it,' she shrieks.

In reality, of course, she defended him to the grave. I, for my part, have never defended anybody. I have only condemned. I am no Colin Chatterton.

Christ, this sounds like an excerpt from Dickens. Did he really do those things to her? I can no longer be one hundred per cent certain, of course. The intervening years have doubtless added colour to specific details, and once all those first things are out of the way, a kind of amnesia sets in.

Seven

Kevin was mute as I propelled the BMW down the winding lanes on the night in question, just stared into the path of the headlights, as if he'd known what was on my mind. Splayed out in his seat there, he smelt earthy and uncouth - a mixture of cancerous bracken and horse droppings, stale sweat and unwashed clothing. He had terrible teeth, Kev; a stranger to flossing. Yellow canines and tinged gums, foul deposits down every divide, the consistency of peanut butter.

It had been, all things considered, a disastrous weekend up to that point. First the attempted mugging, which I had mentioned to nobody, and then Liz Armstrong's visit. Afterwards, as my wife slept in a stupor into the early evening, my son suckling the leaking wine from her breasts, I suffered the body-blow of discovering the portrait of *him* amongst my cherished collection of images on the wall in the toilet.

In an attempt to distract myself, I took the blue folder Liz had left from the darkened lounge to the study, but found myself unable to concentrate on its contents. Then, on returning to the lounge and switching the light on, I discovered my Dire Straits CDs all over the carpet and I knew it was him. They were the straw that broke the camel's back.

I've always liked Dire Straits, such a distinctive, relaxing sound. I can't say I really get on with much modern music though.

When we reached Tom Sedgwick's place I told Kevin what was to happen to him. An appeal to my better nature could have saved him but it was not forthcoming. He had shown no remorse, not a trace of it. One glimmer would have got him off the hook. I let him out, opened Tom's gate and allowed him to make a bolt for it. I knew that's what he'd do, in fact I was banking on it. No backbone, you see. That was that.

Sunday morning, as a modern family, we went to *Crazy Capers*, a fun pub for the under-fives, where James Junior could bounce and hit and scream and climb and fall in his stocking feet as we drank foul, overpriced coffee and I attempted to read the papers. Young girls in sports shirts prowled like warders between the webbed play areas, pushing infants into seas of day-glo plastic balls and hoisting them onto vinyl cushions.

'You don't talk to me,' Sally said, as *I'm the King of the Swingers* boomed above the general bedlam.

'I'm sorry?'

'You don't talk to me. At all. About anything.'

She looked puffy and fragile, her leather coat wrapped around her shoulders, hair as usual, a wild tangle of spikes and flattened patches.

'What do you want to talk about?' I asked brightly.

I glanced up from my paper at a cardboard cut-out of a freckled boy with a back-to-front baseball cap on his head. *You can play in here if you're as small as me.*

'I don't mean now.'

'You don't want to talk now?'

'Yes of course I do.'

'About what?'

'I don't know.'

'That's not a theme, as such, is it? Perhaps it is. What don't you know?'

'Why did you marry me?'

King of the Swingers segued into the *Thunderbirds* theme tune and from the nearest tangle of netting, two tots discovered that by falling onto a pair of vinyl wedges they could trigger relentless scattershots of pre-recorded drums. James Junior was up on the second level, his head popping from time to time from behind a livid punch-bag or a lime mushroom.

'I could say I don't know, but then that would only be stretching the idea,' I bellowed, wincing at the noise.

'Why, though?'

I put down the newspaper and looked at her.

'What do you imagine Liz has got that you haven't?'

'What's it got to do with Liz?'

'Everything. That's what she does to people. Makes them dissatisfied. That's what she is. That's why you're being like this, isn't it? Because of her.'

'No.'

'So you're cutting the line of communication then, now, because it doesn't suit you? Is that it? You wanted to talk. You want me to talk like somebody else, that's the point isn't it? To be somebody else. Or perhaps you wish you were somebody else?'

'I want to know what you do,' Sal said, 'what you think about.'

'Why?'

'Because I'm supposed to be your wife. We have to share.'

'We do,' I replied, unconvincingly.

Thankfully, at that point, James Junior came bouncing up, demandingly, and then a voice over the tannoy announced we had served our time.

On returning home, however, Kevin's absence was immediately noticed. Sally spent the afternoon trudging from house to house in the neighbourhood, James Junior confused and tearful at his mother's anxiousness, in a papoose on her back. She tried all his familiar haunts, shouting his name down the ginnels of the dispossessed and the fields of the forlorn, her distress increasing as every hour away from Kev passed. It was quite sickening. Tom finally called in the evening, tears in his eyes.

'I 'ad to shoot 'im, James,' he told us, 'there were nowt else for it. There he were boundin' abart after me rams. Scaring 'em witless and rolling in their shit. I 'ad to shoot 'im.'

Poor old Tom with his batwing eyebrows and his orange peel cheeks was genuinely upset. The thought of him makes me nostalgic for the simple folk of the village just outside Wakefield, where Sally and I settled, her family having lived in the area for generations, and her father being the custodian of its history. My own family had connections with the place of course, with the mill being there.

Tom and his ilk managed to retain a rural innocence whilst having all the benefits of a large city just ten minutes away. Bumpkins, in short. After putting down newspaper on the kitchen tiles, I let him into the house. I poured him a whisky and he slumped onto the sofa still wearing his clay-caked duffel, the peasant. It was Sally I was worried about. I couldn't gauge her reaction. For a moment, I honestly thought she was worried about Tom getting the furniture dirty.

'I don't understand,' she said blankly. I put a consoling arm on her shoulder, but she shrugged me away.

'I knew he were pedigree and tha probably paid a ton for 'im,' Tom continued, 'ther good dogs, 'untin' dogs, burra bit scatty offen.'

It's a complete fallacy that a dog is a man's best friend. When I complained to colleagues that Kevin had it in for me they would palm me off with excuses. It was just his nature, I was told, after discovering my mail had been tampered with to the extent that I began to suspect Kevin kept cross-indexed charts in order to ascertain what correspondence was personally important to me. He kept similar files on my preference in food before selectively raiding the fridge. I was expected to shrug off a lap full of urine as a fond greeting. I knew different.

Imagine if babies were all born hyperactive and weighing in at around six stones each. Imagine if they immediately started ripping up carpets and shitting in potted plants before progressing to savaging pensioners and indiscriminate theft. The population would soon dive significantly.

I didn't say any of this to Sally, of course.

'How did he get so far away?' she demanded, looking suspiciously at me.

'Poor thing,' was all I could manage to utter, 'poor, poor thing.'

Later that night she left me for good.

Eight

Voluntary, if not wilful, amnesia, is the only way I can describe it now, this forgetting of essential details and hankering after first things which are frozen into exaggerated significance.

I can pinpoint the exact time and place it all started: on the front pew of a church, turning to look at a man sitting next to me.

He was in full morning dress as, it became apparent when I glanced down at myself, was I. To our left were full rows of over made-up women in elaborate hats, dabbing at their lips with paper tissues, rustling in handbags and whispering behind battered hymn books, and stiff-collared men collectively generating a sonorous wave of clearing throats, flicking at lapels and creases.

Behind us, however, was a vast expanse of emptiness.

The concealed organist struck up a booming fugue and I turned again to examine the man at my side. I knew he was the 'best man', my best man, but the thing was, who was he? I thought I had probably known him at university, earlier than that perhaps, but suddenly there seemed nothing I could force into my mind about his relationship to myself. Remembering his name was the least of my problems; first I had to colour him, it seemed, with some significance, a detail at least, however trivial. His jacket, I noticed, was a little small, straining at the shoulders, with the skewed buttonhole dangling precariously from his lapel. He was pale and bleary, red-rimmed and bordering on the agitated, over-aftershaved, but nevertheless giving off a faint odour of vomit, my best man. Wide of pupil.

Had we embarked on some wild adventure, he and I, which had resulted in me being pumped with hallucinogenic drugs in some multistorey car-park, on what is referred to as a 'Stag Night'? Did this account for my current predicament?

He patted me on the shoulder so that I saw, to my horror, a tattoo emerging from the cuff of his white shirt. Who would I know with a tattoo? Who, for that matter, did I know who could be called upon to carry out the role of best man for me?

Were there agencies, I wondered, where such people could be hired for the day, like escorts, or kissograms?

He patted my shoulder again, and I froze.

Then it struck me there were other things I should remember. I was marrying a girl called Sally. Of that I was certain. But who was she? How long had I known her? What did she look like? Had we had sex yet, or was she saving herself? Presumably I had proposed, and if so, when, and how? Did I get down on a bended knee in some restaurant, or was the occasion more muted, curled on a sofa, perhaps, walking along a beach? This seemed unlikely. Had I presented her with a ring? Had we discussed our future together? What were our plans?

In my panic, as the organist pumped out *The Wedding March* and the stained glass saints stared down, I vowed I would ask myself no more questions. I would assert facts; state what I knew and let the rest fall into place.

This was my wedding day. It was a white wedding, in a church. Sally was who I was getting married to. She would look all white. The city could have been Wakefield, or York. Not York, this wasn't the Minster. I had probably known Sally for at least as long as I had known the best man who was sitting next to me. We must have hired our clothes at a shop together.

My father would not be coming. Sally's father was a historian, and would know about this cathedral we were in, the tribulations of its clergy, the vision of its designers and the exertion of those who laboured on it; what was here before it existed. And perhaps I had discussed seating arrangements and flowers and place-mats with him, or his wife, who wore multicoloured leggings, despite her age.

I glanced back at the empty pews, at an invisible family, as Sally and her father loomed towards us down the aisle. And then the ceremony was underway and I was standing at her side sandwiched by amber-cheeked teenagers, bridesmaid cousins in pearl satin and taffeta. Unfortunately my bride was wearing a veil which kept her identity a mystery to me. The delicate lace constructions of her dress and train did, however, bring to mind certain slender items of lingerie I thought I might have seen her in. But these could have been modelled by someone else.

I followed the clergyman's lips - was he vicar, priest? What was the distinction? - his eyelids flickering their own morse code, until it came to the part where we kissed, and her face and lips, to my utter relief, proved themselves vaguely familiar once revealed. Though no more than that.

Outside, as the bells clanged and the assembled showered us with confetti, she said, 'I won't forgive the old bastard for this. I feel sorry for you more than anything.'

As we climbed into the Rolls Royce, she said, 'I only hope he's proud of himself, that's all. His only son.'

The photographs took place in the grounds of the hotel where the reception was later held, and throughout the proceedings more details emerged, through the clenched-teeth mutterings of my new wife.

The best man turned out to be her brother, Alan, so the escort agency idea was not that far from the truth. My father, it seemed, had taken exception to the marriage, for reasons which were unclear, although I was dimly aware of listening to a long litany of invective concerning men who preferred books to hard work and sloth being genetic, but by that time he was not fully *compos mentis*. A week later however, he upstaged the ceremony thrown by the Gittings at which he refused to be present, by posting to us the keys to the house here in Wakefield, in which we duly set up home.

The location of our honeymoon was probably exotic.

Nine

Once Tom had tearfully crocodiled out into the night, having imparted the tragic news about Kevin, and doubtless intent on further drowning his sorrows in whatever sawdust and spittoon farming labourer's saloon he regularly scattered and spat in, Sally and I argued.

Not, it has to be said, for anything like the first time, but I suppose in my anxiety I must have drunk more than usual, since the following morning, when I awoke at my desk in the study, the entire text had been erased. The thrusts of our arguments, the gists and the grists of our respective grievance lists, the spiteful sparring, the tears, threats and recriminations, all were lost. The only thing that remained was a nauseous kernel, a painful intuition. This was a combination of general hostility, the perpetual crying of James Junior, and a long, uncomfortable sleep disturbed by mysterious bumps in the night; by barks and scratching and scraping, rather as if I'd been sleeping in the cabin of a ship during a savage storm.

I had the distinct impression of intense turbulence: squalls blasting the double glazing, the wind rattling at the pipes and water pumping from the gutters, gusts spiralling down the chimney and through the eaves.

I was surprised however, on opening the blinds, to find that the garden revealed no traces of elemental carnage, that the fences were not flattened and the borders were not demolished, the bird pool was not overflowing and the lawn hadn't been converted to swamp. Instead, a weak late-autumn sun dribbled across the still, surrounding fields.

I knew by then to ignore the feeling of unease I generally awoke with, since the majority of the irritating little phrases which had wormed their way into my mind and taken on monstrous implications had never actually been uttered; they were some kind of alcohol-induced alternative to wish-fulfilment. Nevertheless, they swam at me in a vague wave.

As I tried to make sense of the papers strewn in front of me, the telephone exploded from the hall, its accusing tone adding to my discomfort. It reminded me of Sal at her most petulant, when she'd decided to deny me peace and quiet.

I squirmed my way from the swivel chair, pitched and steepled out into the hall, and even before I picked the receiver up, it became apparent that something was wrong.

'James, where are they?'

Liz sounded like an early night, a jog, and a breakfast of muesli and fruit.

'Where are what?'

'The papers I left. You promised they'd be here.'

'Christ, what time is it?'

'Eight thirty.'

I stretched out for the door handle, instinctively knowing it would give. Even in a stupor, I never forgot to lock up. Then I saw the note, a lemon tongue poking at me from the letterbox.

Sally's handwriting was childish, full of flowery circles and exclamation marks. Though I can't say I ever saw them, I bet the borders of her schoolbooks were overgrown, thick with felt-tip petals and buds.

'James? Are you there?'

'I'll drop them in on the way to court. Stop hassling me, okay?'

I put the phone down on her, leaving the receiver off the hook, and taking Sally's letter back through to the study.

For some reason she'd considered it important to let me know how to operate the washing machine, when to water the plants and what to tell the domestic, before letting rip with the invective.

She would not remain married to anyone capable of saying what I'd said, she wrote, failing to provide me with anything resembling a prompt to my memory, nor would she allow her child to be fathered by same.

By the time I got to the lines about Kevin and hearing from her solicitor her squirls and squorls had given way to an uneven, gothic script which made me wonder if she might be schizophrenic.

I put the note down and bundled up all the papers on the desk, wedging them back into Liz's folder. There was also a stack of unopened letters I should really have dealt with over the weekend. These were in the main from such companies as Amex, Visa and Chargecard, along with numerous banks and investment agencies, all of them rather irritatingly marked urgent. If all were equally so, to which was I supposed to give priority?

I carried everything through into the lounge, to be confronted by chaos. The place had been ransacked. The fine china and porcelain was gone, as were the television, video and CD-stack, the Regency dining table and its chairs, the rugs and tapestries, my father's pair of clarinets - even the two cut glass chandeliers. Drawers had been emptied out and the discarded remains left on the carpet - chewed biros and clumps of tissue, envelopes and paper clips. Sunlight cleaved the room apart - even the curtains were missing.

'Sally?' I called out, uncertainly.

In the kitchen, the sink was still heaped with dirty crockery, but the contents of the cupboards had been pillaged. At intervals around the work surfaces stood opened cans of beer and split packets of crisps. Quite a party, obviously.

It struck me at that point that Sally's moonlight flit accounted for my disturbed sleep. I realised she couldn't have moved all those things on her own, and I was given reason to dislike her tight-knit family even more than I had previously.

Tidying up as best I could, I tried to picture the scene. The presence of her brother, my 'best man', Alan, with his tattooed wrists, would account for the kitchen snacks.

A proper family affair, it must have been: ravaging with black bin-liners, humping on tiptoe.

Glancing at my watch I realised with alarm that I was due in court in less than ten minutes' time and hurriedly began dressing and gathering together my papers, some of which had been tossed to the carpet in my wife's cloak and dagger midnight activities. It wasn't until I stepped out into the hall and searched for my keys that it became apparent she'd taken the car too.

Ten

I did not go to pieces after Sally left. I was convinced her departure represented nothing more than a brief hiatus, but in any case became quickly acclimatised to a comfortable solitude. And at the same time I thought about the firsts. The first sex, music, book, meal, alcohol; what they meant. I saw that I had fallen into a lifestyle that was all weary habit and that even if I couldn't recapture them, I had to seek out some first things again, to sharpen blunted edges.

It was, in any case, a matter of pride with me that I never relied on a woman to iron me a shirt or cook me a meal. Not, I might add, out of any misplaced notion of equality, but simply because I could do such things with more care and attention to detail myself. And perhaps in memory of my mother. I could eat when and what I wanted to, and study my case files without constant interruption. I would also, I felt sure, become less inclined to reach for the bottle the moment I stepped over the threshold.

I was a little relieved that Sally had seen fit to undertake the systematic stripping of our previously cluttered rooms. I revelled in the almost Japanese austerity which was the result. At the same time I was angered at her decision to take certain things she was aware were of great sentimental value, and had been in our family for generations. These, I vowed, not least my father's clarinets, I would reclaim if she actually wasn't coming back.

It was also during those brief days of space and clarity however, that I finally got around to attending to all those unopened letters and discovered our financial situation to be less than healthy. As a family unit we had, it seemed, been falling through the holes in our pockets. It became apparent that with the possibility of divorce arising I would be required to take a tight hold on the reins, in preparation for the switches Sally's solicitors would inevitably apply to my financial rear.

Much of my rightful inheritance was still tied up in my father's business interests and it seemed to me these should, by and large, be left to their own devices, not least the mill. I was beginning to find Liz Armstrong's attitude irksome, which was why the phone remained off the hook. Having given her more or less carte blanche in the running of the business and all associated interests, I was at a loss as to why I should be constantly bothered for my approval in matters I neither knew nor cared anything about. Especially since it seemed she had now assumed the right to call on me direct, pushing her way into my life with all the blatant nonchalance of my mugger friend, Ronald Pickles. The last thing I needed was another of those tedious meetings with her, although I knew if I didn't do something about the contents of the blue folder she'd left with me, it was inevitable.

I picked it up and gingerly leafed out a few examples of its contents.

The mill was, as far as I was aware, still a vastly profitable remnant of my father's empire, mainly because it had always been run on strict authoritarian lines, employing only the wives of those at the bottom of the pile who couldn't find work elsewhere, in Victorian conditions. As a sort of sleeping MD, which is what I considered myself, it would have been conceivable for me to have improved things, but of course I didn't, for reasons of both profit, and tradition.

Women were employed because they worked harder and for less money, grateful to escape their kids and their pokey houses, most of which were built by my grandfather. In a way, working in the mill was their recreation. Perhaps we should have applied for government aid considering the useful social service we were providing. The women were, on the whole, by no means past it, but they did convincing impersonations of the ruined and abandoned, with their knife and fork hairstyles and cave paint, their skiv aprons and bronchial chests. They'd split open the bales and rummage through the pockets of old clothes, grateful for the odd note they might find. Not averse to unclogging oily drains, inhaling poisonous fumes or braving arctic or tropical conditions, they'd do anything they were told to with a baffling form of compliant complaint; with skull-splitting, four-letter submission.

They took their work very seriously, spending their breaks discussing the intricacies of compressing quilts or stuffing pillows, when they were not chirping about the kids they'd so desperately escaped from.

To me, and to my father and Liz Armstrong too, they epitomised everything that was terrifying about having no money. They knew to the exact penny the prices of the bare essentials, their minds cluttered with shopping lists and check-out chits. Their time was too important to be squandered on simple pleasure and their timekeeping would have been considered supernatural by advertising executives or merchant bankers. They turned up even in illness. Sickness benefit wasn't paid anyway for short-term contract, part-time workers, and every hour was another Superloaf and a tin of beans, a packet of disposable nappies or a beer in the husband's belly. They had no memory of the first anything. Complete amnesia.

Those husbands, God, those husbands. They were nameless and interchangeable, rednecks ringed with the woad of a backstreet needle, nicotine-bleached ham-fists adept at the blistering backhander. He didn't really like her working but His employment was seasonal; He liked to go down to the club for the dominoes on Friday (they couldn't afford it really but it got Him out of the house); He had fines to pay, or time to serve; His mates were always in trouble but He wasn't bad really. The unspoken conclusion reached was that He would do anything to escape, and she would have been much better off without Him.

Yes, I'm sorry to say that these women were exploited for every last penny. The hourly rate was well below the recommended minimum, but then again, everyone else got away with it. The place had to be competitive, Liz Armstrong would point out, echoing my father beyond the grave. We were competing with Thailand and Tunisia and Pakistan where life was much cheaper, and we were not in business creating jobs and prosperity for all, just for the fun of it. There was a compulsory overtime scheme in operation, which had the effect of cancelling out the bonus payments they strived so hard to secure. The bonus system itself verged on the illegal, with no allowance made for breakdown times or coffee breaks. If anybody reached a performance target it was instantly increased. God only knows what it must have been like in the adjoining chemical place, where life-threatening contaminations also figured in the equation.

I knew the Wakefield mill well enough, since a couple of my teenage summers had been spent there, if not exactly in gainful employment then near enough to it to convince my father I was making myself useful, and was at the same time safe under his beady eye.

Liz Armstrong was there then, only a few years older than me, scurrying about the place to meet my father's demands, a pale shadow of her future self.

Summers inside that place, it got so hot. The dust scalded your nostrils and the bleach and fibres cracked your flesh. When the buzzing of the compressors stopped, the flies would echo them, swooping in clusters on discarded paper cups and crisp bags. Below, on the ground floor, the conveyors creaked like the stairs of haunted houses and the looms dived and crashed.

Stripped to the waist, I did the jobs the women considered beneath them. Not for me the frantic bagging, the insect-like scurrying, the piston-like gyrations. They would allow me to order their sandwiches, say, or mark down their output rates on scraps of card. Occasionally I would help fold a few sheets or drag a broom down an aisle. Mostly I just watched, making them feel uncomfortable.

But did they resent my privileged position? Of course not. They respected it. Their own offspring would have been sent to Coventry for such tardiness; dispatched to Hell and back, strapped to the conveyor belt naked with their balls coated in axle grease. Not me. I was mothered and sheltered from the harsh reality of their lives. I can't say I blame them for wanting to conceal it from me. I was probably the nearest they'd ever come to royalty. They toned down the swearing and the smutty talk for my ears, brought me ointments to put on my skin when it became inflamed and showed tender concern when the dust troubled my sinuses.

But the second year I was there something had changed. There was a detectable drop in the atmosphere. Detectable, that is, to an educated sensibility. I doubt the women were aware of it.

I myself had changed; sprouted into an awkward impersonation of a man with a face full of yellowheads and a voice fluctuating between Lee Marvin and Mickey Mouse, complexion and vocal chords refusing to walk in straight lines. I had ceased, temporarily, to be loveable. I started to detect hostility as, slouched in the canteen with the radio glued to my ear, I watched the women at their labours. I wasn't scared of hard work, as was cautiously implied more than once. I had simply come to the conclusion that it wasn't for me.

And then my Parker pen went missing. I couldn't understand it, since I never left it lying around. It was gold-nibbed, with my signature inscribed in leaf along the side. When my father got wind of this he arranged an instant search of his employees. This didn't produce the pen. Neither did an hour of haranguing and the threat of docked wages.

Posters were put up throughout the factory offering a handsome reward for anonymous information leading to the detection of the thief. The atmosphere became strained, a breaking of the ranks led to uncertainty, suspicion and rumour. Concealed hostilities bubbled to the surface.

I had an idea who'd taken it. There was one woman who I'd never warmed to, and the feeling seemed to be mutual.

Pam Riley wasn't popular, despite the fact that she deserved sympathy for being married to a drunken milkman who constantly beat her up and had given her a kid with chronic asthma. There was something about Pam that made you, if not exactly sympathise with her husband, then at least understand him. The emanation of fear often provokes an extreme reaction, the primal instinct being to go immediately for the jugular. I felt sorry for the kid, though. His life seemed to be an endless round of fevered nights and doctor's waiting rooms, injections and excuse notes.

The others should have told Pam about her personal hygiene problem, but instead they mockingly turned up their noses behind her back and complained to the foreman that she wasn't pulling her weight.

About a week after the pen went missing, a routine end of shift security search at the clock machine revealed Pam's carrier bag to be a veritable Aladdin's cave. Stowed in the folds of her overall were rolls of sellotape, a pair of scissors, cotton reels and a cask of industrial soap. The thief exposed, the rest of the employees breathed a collective sigh of relief and everything went back to normal.

Where will Pam Riley be now? Does she still live in the shadow of the mill with her brute husband and sick kid? The kid will be old enough to beat her up too by now, a tribal twoccer, well-rehearsed ramraider and glue-sniffing graduate. Did she ever work again after that fall from grace, I wonder?

I was convinced, beyond a shadow of a doubt, that Pam had my pen, but my conviction would not have sufficed to bring about hers. She was certainly a cool customer. I watched her very closely as she stood in line with the others, being humiliated and threatened by my father. Her face had never twitched, there was not a trace of guilt in those limpid eyes behind their bottleglass shields. Perhaps she'd had other things on her mind.

The problem with the law in this country is that it often allows the guilty to walk free by dint of some obscure loophole or technicality. The case for the prosecution has to be watertight. Any sign of irregularity, any doubt allowed to be sown in the minds of the jury, is a gift to the defence.

By putting the things in Pam's bag I was merely trying to see justice done, nothing more than that.

Funnily enough, the pen turned up a few weeks later, in a pair of jeans my mother had foolishly allowed to slip behind the laundry basket.

Eleven

Once I'd written a long letter to Liz Armstrong I felt much better. I outlined all my reasons for wanting to withdraw my capital from the business set up by my father and requiring a settlement figure, which would include all shareholder incentives and bonuses, compensation for fringe benefits and accumulated interests, to be deposited with me as a matter of urgency.

It gave me a degree of satisfaction, I admit, to imagine Armstrong opening my letter and grappling with the implications, doubtless seeing towers of figures teetering and toppling in her head, the bailiffs swooping on the fixtures and fittings, a large *Closed* sign across the rusting gates of the mill and the test tubes of those chemists trembling. Feet of clay, her associates would conclude.

But Liz and the others surely couldn't have expected to be propped up by Turner money forever, and I assumed they would have laid contingency plans. If not, then they really didn't deserve to be standing in my father's boots. Diligently, I went through the documents in the blue folder, putting my mark against the red crosses Liz had marked for me. After all, I wasn't being awkward, just wanting what I was entitled to. As a last word I stapled together all of the bills from those credit companies and scrawled a note to the effect that I'd like them to be settled on my behalf, sooner rather than later, from what was owed to me. As a gesture of intent.

The next morning, as I pushed the package through the door of the mill's reception, I bumped into old Franklin, dangling his keys. He put a liver-spotted hand on my shoulder and started to breathe heavily, as if recovering from a race.

'James,' he said, 'good to see you boy.'

'Thought you were on holiday, Franklin.'

'Holiday? Not me. Your father never was one for holidays either. It pains me, James, pains me to see what's going on here these days. These young ones with their fancy ways. Throwing it about hand-over-fist. Well it doesn't grow on trees. He'd never have stood for it. I remember...'

'Franklin, I haven't time now,' I cut him dead, striding off briskly. 'Shanks's pony at the moment, marital dispute.'

He was still standing gawping after me, the keys in his hand, when I glanced back from the top of the road.

For the rest of that week I threw myself wholeheartedly into my work, expecting to return home to find all manner of anxious messages awaiting me, having reconnected, and feeling rather deflated by the mute flicker from the barren answer-phone. But I immersed myself in taking on more than my share of that surplus butter mountain which is the Crown's backlog of pending prosecutions, resharpening the dry rapier of my wit and rediscovering, to my delight, my adeptness at advocacy.

I suppose it was in the nature of my profession to be suspicious, and sometimes to expect the worst in people. Unfortunately - as the bulging files I was obliged to tow to the courts bore out - they were usually happy to live down to my expectations.

I saw more than enough in those few days however, of Colin Chatterton, who seemed to be single-handedly championing every lost cause in West Yorkshire. On Wednesday we dined together with the magistrates, and although the company was too restrained to say as much, he rather embarrassed us all by his insistence on talking shop.

Magistrates are, of course, quite entitled to take into account the solitary impulse of the sneak-thief, the dependency of the drug dealer and sometimes even the genuine remorse of a rapist or near-murderer. But they certainly shouldn't be expected to do so while attempting to appreciate exquisitely-presented roast beef platters and a 1989 claret.

Chatterton, his elbows on the table and the napkin pushed crudely into his frayed shirt front, pressed home point after point, oblivious to the throat clearances, vacant stares and attempts to change the subject.

They seemed to listen sincerely enough to his reiteration of straight-and-narrow promises, the pleas of peer pressure, deprivation and desperation on behalf of his clients, but I sensed it rather put the mockers on things. Then, as we were poised to devour a collectively-chosen house specialité - aromatic sticky pudding - he looked at his watch and announced that court was set to resume in less than five minutes. Just as I was about to berate him for his rudeness, the chief magistrate dabbed his raw cheeks, and rising, said that Chatterton was quite correct, and we should observe our civic duty. As we filed out, pulling coats from the backs of chairs around the linen and silver spread containing full dishes and half-empty bottles, he shot me a sly look of self-satisfaction.

Then, on Friday morning he had a peculiar run of luck - a brace of suspended sentences, a community service order and a handful of fines which amounted to the state punishing itself. Nothing went the Crown's way. When the magistrates retired for lunch again, I busied myself with my files, rather than having to exchange the affirmation of our professional distance I sensed Chatterton was hovering for.

When he left, I bought Sergeant Dick Woolin a coffee from the dispenser and we slumped onto the olive vinyl of the bench in the deserted waiting room, as a gowned clerk emptied the ash-trays frostily.

'They think I'm paid to be the cleaner too,' she said, before stomping off.

'Another one out the window,' I complained to Woolin. 'What a shower.'

'Tell me about it,' he replied, leafing absently through a coverless motoring magazine. Woolin had been made to look quite ridiculous by Chatterton that morning, as he read evidence from his notebook in respect of a compulsive teenage car thief who should have been sent down.

'Doesn't it piss you off, having to go through all that, knowing he can just twist anything you say, jump in at any point? Make you look stupid?'

He shrugged, still immersed in the magazine.

'Gets me off the streets.'

'That's the spirit,' I replied, with more disdain than I intended.

'You think I'm joking?' He glanced across at me, then resumed reading. 'Anyway, it's all a bit of a game, isn't it? I don't mind the likes of Col Chatterton doing that. That's what he's paid for.'

The regular police constables I met in the courts, the 'turnip tops' as they are known, I found to be quite keen on being given the wherewithal to properly tackle crime. Reared on *Robocop* and *Die Hard*, they wanted the trappings of our brothers and allies across the pond: the quasars that would produce enough voltage to floor a buffalo on crack at twenty yards, flak jackets, the tear gas and mace, leaded night-sticks and armoured cars, fire-power for the thin blue line. They wanted the birch and the rope, and to be asked no questions for acting on their inside knowledge and hunches. Zero tolerance. Ammunition.

At least they had enthusiasm. This Woolin, however, was older, more experienced. Resigned to it all.

'Did you think he'd get off with it? The twoccer?'

He took a sip from the plastic cup, grimaced, and glanced up again, as if surprised at his surroundings.

'That is absolutely vile. Yes, I knew he would. We're only talking about a nuisance, aren't we? A young pest, stealing cars. Taking without care and consideration. Twoccing. That sounds almost sweet. To be honest I don't really care. My shift's done in twenty minutes, and I'm not rushing back.'

'That shower though,' I said, 'it's always the same. Moan constantly about the breakdown of society and the inability of you lot to catch criminals. Then when you do...'

'They want to go back to tugged forelocks and doors left on the latch,' Woolin replied. 'When criminals could be relied on to come clean when collared and accept their punishment with good grace. Don't we all. But if you think I looked stupid, what about you?'

'What?'

'They were listening out of politeness, that's all.'

It was true, I realised. More often than not, they looked across to the dock and saw nothing of a pensioner's terror, a small shopkeeper's ruin, a nurse's dismay. They buried their heads ostrich-like in the sand rather than face up to the frenzied forces of wilful destruction. This implied I was not doing my job properly, that my words were not coming alive. They saw children, much like their own - children to be given a symbolic clip around the ear and stood in the corner - as if their duties amounted to nothing more than a display of headmasterly severity. Colin Chatterton was successfully acting as the Pied Piper to those 'children' - dancing them gleefully down the path of chaos and disorder.

'Don't think we don't get pissed off about it,' Woolin said, rising to his feet. 'We do.' He threw the magazine down on the bench. 'An afternoon on the allotment for me now, anyway, get it all out of my head. Thanks for the coffee. It was foul.'

He left, to be replaced by a cleaner, hauling a vacuum like a disobedient dog behind her and spraying the air with the scent of apples.

The police took it personally. Most of them. Woolin was an exception. They would scowl and gnaw their knuckles, awaiting the outcome of whatever David and Goliath situation had forced them to pit all their guile against the massed ranks of social workers, defence solicitors, professional counsellors and voluntary advisors, youth team leaders, probation officers, predatory pressmen and 'community representatives'. Not to mention the love-blindness of the parents and wives, in alignment with the unblinking nonchalance of the accused themselves.

I never felt the slightest remorse about convincing the magistrates to convict wrongdoers for crimes I knew they hadn't committed. The crimes were often interchangeable, as were the criminals - as indeed were the representatives of the law and the lawbreakers - the convictions were all that counted. It was a question of duty.

I did however, on more occasions than I can remember, feel I had let individual policemen down, in not getting convictions. Often, it was like watching a meticulously constructed matchstick model being demolished with a single hammer-blow. The legwork and attention to detail, the late nights spent in unsavoury company, the stress and frequent danger of criminal scenes, the drawn-out arresting procedure, the hours of paperwork, the endless questioning, the domestic tension, the checking and re-checking of notebooks, the anxiety of awaiting the arrival of key witnesses - all felled with one swoop.

Those witnesses of course were often unwilling to come forward at all, fearing a brick through the window, or coins across the car paintwork, vendettas, retribution. The public would bray for blood, condemn the police and swallow all the misinformation and hyperbole about the unfairness of our legal system. But they wouldn't dirty their hands. And we were all, unfortunately - those of us involved - elbow deep in the contents of the darkest drain.

'Come on, love,' the cleaner with her apple spray said, finally, releasing me from my meditation. 'Haven't you got a home to go to?'

I walked home, seeing nothing. The house suddenly felt empty.

I'd heard nothing from my wife or her solicitors for a full working week, and though well aware that such things took time to set in motion, I couldn't prevent the occasional flutter of optimism from taking hold of me, as if somehow everything would be all right.

Then, for want of distraction, I pulled out a file from my case and was drawn with more than professional interest to its subjects, emblazoned on the cover:

R Pickles and J Raven

The first being, of course, the mugger I'd had the misfortune to mug.

Twelve

The Righteous Brother, Trevor says they call me, the name having been coined by one of the gang of older West Indian guys in here. He says I put them in mind of the severe preachers some were subjected to as children, and he detects a sly admiration. Having said that, they'd all happily stab me soon as look at me. Their dominoes resonate around the cells as they're slapped down on the ping-pong table of the recreation room, accompanied by piercing exclamations and throaty laughter. The younger ones stick together as much as they can, rolling like a wave of shoulders around the place, muscles glistening, wide eyes full of mistrust, talking down their sleeves.

But it's the whites I have to watch, he tells me, especially the smackheads, the thin boys with the blotches and dead eyes. He's been on the receiving end of numerous requests, he's said, relishing his power, his role of protector. Just give us a minute with him, they've begged Trevor, thirty seconds even. Long enough to tear some flesh, break a bone or two. Turn your back on the corridor, Trev mate, let a shiv find his 'kin cheek, X marks the spot. Stand him in the right shadow when you're circling the yard, man, so we can drop a boiling pan down, wipe that 'kin law-maker's sneer from his lips.

The ingenuity they are capable of applying to the creation of improvised, debilitating weaponry is nothing short of breathtaking: shampoo or potatoes, shirt cuffs and paper can all be turned into something deadly at the drop of a hat. Preferable though is the concealed and anonymous attack, the shard in the soap or the crushed powders in the soup.

Many of them, it seems, have followed my case from the outset, from that unfortunate outburst on the court steps and what followed, immediately after the Pickles and Raven trial. Having sat through interminable hours of the accusations and moral outrage of men like me, they now want the luxury of judging, to redefine themselves from a loftier position. It's why the nonces get it, this insatiable desire to slip from the frame and put someone else at its centre.

Then again, they'd be just as happy to inflict the damage on a grey-haired granny or a telephone box, I just happen to be in the immediate line of fire.

'But I don't see why they should have the satisfaction,' Trevor told me proudly as he entered my cell first thing this morning, 'not on my shift anyway.'

What walking contradictions they are, prison officers.

'Your problem Mister Turner,' he said, 'is that you're a symbol.'

He winked as he imparted this vital information, setting down a breakfast tray - shrivelled cereal husks in watery milk, an enamel vat of brown tea - at the side of my mattress.

'A symbol of what, exactly?' I asked wearily.

'Of everything that's wrong out there.'

I shrugged and spooned in some cereal, anxious neither to offend nor encourage him.

'It's fine for the politicians,' he continued, 'they can just shrug it off when they're caught with their fingers in the till, but I was brought up to believe politeness was paramount. Don't you think so?'

'Surely.'

'Manners maketh the man, was the way my dad had it, and I was happy to follow in his footsteps down these corridors.'

I like Trevor. All spit and polish he is, glistening fob, patent caps and brilliantine, white socks and razor creases, the tabloid he brings for me rolled up and clenched under his armpit like a baton.

'No, my problem,' he said, 'is I like people, and these days it's just not fashionable.'

I met his eyes at that point, expecting to see them twinkling with irony, but realising he was serious.

'If I was a social worker you'd cringe at that,' he continued, 'and I wouldn't bloody blame you, but I'm just a screw, and I can put my hand on my heart and honestly say I've never met anybody I didn't like, one way or another.'

He glanced furtively out along the corridor, poking his head back in to my cell and lowering his voice to a conspiratorial whisper.

'I'll tell you one thing,' he continued, 'what's wonderful, what really says it all about human nature, is that nobody is truly evil, don't you think?'

I shrugged, at a loss for words.

'It's true!' he barked, spreading his arms expansively. 'They all strive essentially to be good, every last man-jack-boy. I've never held anything against anybody, certainly not for more than twenty-four hours.' He sniffed and straightened his back with a hint of pride. 'You see Mister Turner, there are always redeeming features to be found that more than compensate for your behavioural flaws or your personality failures. I like people for that alone, me, and I'm not blowing my own trumpet here, just recognising something I can do nothing about.'

'Are you quite sure about that?' I asked, spooning in another mouthful of the cereal, feeling it cement itself to my palate and worm its way between fillings.

Trevor crouched at my side at this point, smelling of toothpaste and hair-oil and institutional mock-freshness.

'Of course I'm sure.'

He let his arms quickly flourish, as if conducting an invisible orchestra, partly grasping for the idea, partly finding his balance. It was a gesture which reminded me, in its striving for expression, of my son, at the age of about nine months.

'Deadly sins,' he said, 'the seven. Revenge, take that, for instance, just as an example.'

'Take revenge then,' I agreed.

'It's a concept outside my conception, that's all I'm saying.'

'Really,' I said, not able to hide my amusement at the turn our conversation was taking.

'It's true.' He clicked his heels. 'One hundred percent. Greed, I admit to, and envy, and of course, your lust. But only fleetingly. If anything, these failings, these so-called deadly sins, could be seen as confirmation of my inability to dislike people.'

'But how, Trevor? You're losing me.'

'Well,' - he was getting quite excited now - 'my greed, envy and lust all amount to one and the same thing as I see it.'

'Which is?'

He waited for effect, savouring his moment.

'Homage.' A flourish of his hand, like a magician.

'Homage?'

'Of course they are!' He sighed, as if suspecting me of being deliberately obstinate. 'How, how is it possible to be greedy without respecting the qualities others have and you lack? To be greedy is to believe in the future, surely, to seek self-improvement? How can you envy what you don't admire, how lust after something you don't want?'

He paused, and with a creaking in his throat I don't think he was aware of, took a long draught of my tea.

'I'll tell you one thing,' he said then, 'a total stranger could approach me, in a bar, say, and tell me about his life. I would only have his word for it, for whatever part of his experience, his longing, his self-delusion, he chose to put through the mental bloody mincer and hand me on a plate, all shredded and bruised. Anybody.'

'Anybody?'

'Anybody.'

'Adolf Hitler, say?'

'Adolf Hitler, of course Adolf Hitler,' he snorted with contempt at the idea. 'I'd stand aside for him to order his drink with a polite smile, I just bloody bet I would, emanating, as you would probably put it, having gone to university, an air of being both approachable and well-mannered. We would drink in silence or he could, should he so wish, produce a faded photo of a bunch of his ruddy cheeked cronies...'

'Or of Eva Braun,' I suggest.

'Or Eva, or a child or a pet, from his wallet, and pour out his black heart like the chorus of a bad country and western song. I'd bloody swallow it, I'm telling you that now. I like people too much not to.'

'It's interesting,' I said to him.

'It is too,' he readily agreed, 'and for that reason, it seems to me that guns are the only way forward.'

Immediately it occurred to me that it is for the best that men like Trevor are behind metre-thick walls and razor wire for much of the time.

He pushed himself to his feet and stared out at the corridor again, suddenly avoiding my eyes completely. He turned to stare at the wall above my head with a beatific expression of contempt.

'The panic aroused by such a prospect baffles me,' he said. 'Utterly and completely, puts me at a loss. Guns are the way back to the time of leaving the door unlocked without fear, of reclaiming the subways and the parks, I'll tell you that. It's not as if the crims don't have their own fucking arsenals already, but....but, the prospect of returning fire would surely put an end to their casual attitude.'

'Nothing's more certain,' I said.

'The bullet would put a halt to any mitigating circumstances wouldn't it? And clear up all the paperwork.'

'But it would just lead to...'

'Fears of anarchy and chaos are just misplaced. Those who took advantage of the system and sought to live by the gun would be afraid to ever sleep. Guns would draw the distinction between Saint Francis and General Franco, or Charles Manson and Mother Teresa, for the people like me who just can't bring themselves to dislike anybody.'

'Well, I don't know.'

He handed me the tabloid. The front page gave lurid details of the latest madman to have run amok with his gun in a supermarket. I patted it for his attention, but he didn't seem to notice.

'Better to have and not need, than to need and not have, they say.' He finally looked at me directly with a smile on lips. 'To which I would add, the muzzle pointed at the man maketh the manners.'

He folded his fist into a gun barrel and peered down imaginary sights with a squint before picking up my tray.

'Well,' he said finally, 'that's my problem: liking everybody. Yours, as I think I've already mentioned, is that you're a symbol. Which is probably the only reason you've got a visitor. And an attractive piece she is too, Mister Turner.'

Thirteen

Raven was not a name unknown to me, one which had, over the years, conspired to dominate enough CPS paper to account for half an Amazonian rain forest. A name, you would think, which would strike fear and trepidation into the hearts of my friend Trevor and his fellow screws.

This however, is not the case at all.

'A character,' Trevor opines, rather as if he were describing some refined man of leisure with a generosity of spirit the equal to that of his wallet, as opposed to a self-opinionated thug the HM Prisons management had moved mountains to distract through such dangling carrots as deep counselling, sociology and unregulated artistic expression. These things failed.

Jimmy Raven had spent more time in prison than out since his teens for nothing very clever: Failed credit card scams and pub protection rackets, sordid love triangles which ended in tears and torn limbs, club clobberings and bungled, booze-addled break-ins.

With his startled features and dishevelled hair he bore a more than passing resemblance to the comedian Tommy Cooper, and when he appeared in court, as he had done often, I couldn't help picturing him with a fez on his head. He was a biter and a gouger, a hit-first, prison-educated pit-bull. Imagine pressing your face against a floor, and then lifting yourself up by the arms again; on tiptoe, with calves rigid. Imagine doing it again. And then again. And then every five seconds from now until the Christmas after the next one. You wouldn't even come close to the time he's spent doing it. His back is ram-rod straight, muscles set like concrete. He's steel-wired like a series of girders, Raven, capable of killing with the back of his hand; with a thrust of his gut; a jut of the chin.

But Trevor will not have a bad word spoken against him.

'He knows the system,' he says, 'respects it. Not like the young ones. He does his time with respect.'

'And then they let him out again,' I retort. 'To treat unfortunate members of the public with disrespect.'

Trevor shrugs at this.

'If he's done his time...'

'Perhaps you should have that gun,' I tell Trevor.

Jimmy Raven was almost famous. Back in the early seventies he'd done a cabaret turn as a sort-of cross between Engelbert Humperdinck and Bernard Manning. 'The Blue Crooner', was how he was billed on the chicken-in-a-basket circuit, and as usual the poor sod didn't understand that the people around him were duping him. He was a freak show unable to distinguish between an audience laughing with him and at him. With his broad frame straining under garish cavalier shirts, his vocal chords would beat up Sinatra songs and his jokes were prefaced by accreditations to popular mass murderers and gangsters. He was the subject of a heavily ironic TV documentary and got stardust in his brain for a while. Until the next human target wandered into his sights. These days he's reported to be in less than the best of health after a run-in with some drug dealers over in Manchester. Too old.

What respect could Ronald Pickles have for him, I wondered? Was it some kind of father-and-son relationship? A Fagin and Dodger situation? I was, I must admit, completely intrigued.

A sub-post office had been robbed, I read, in one of Wakefield's leafier suburbs the previous summer. Its back door had been clubbed through with baseball bats, and the slumbering post master and his wife were dragged from their beds by the two masked men - Fred Flintstone and Barney Rubble - in jogging suits and trainers.

What is it about masks, the appropriation of cartoon or celebrity images, that makes them so fearsome? A combination of the over-familiar in a new and unwelcome context? The mobility of the anonymous eyes in an expanse of rigidity? Or is it something much more rooted to childhood fears, the symbols of safety turning into the stuff of nightmares, the television growing teeth?

As patiently as he could, Jeff Harcross, the postmaster, explained to Fred and Barney that his safe was activated by a timing mechanism which would automatically open in eight hours' time, not before. This did not greatly please the two men. Fred let out a bellow the equal of anything his cartoon counterpart was capable of, and began swinging his club, in Neanderthal fashion, at the photographs and ornaments on the dressing table, at the panels of the wardrobes, at the radio alarm and the bedside lamp. It was long past last orders, no chance of a lock-in down at The Wool Scourer, after all.

Barney then somehow managed to placate his hot-headed buddy. They left the room, but returned moments later. They tied and taped Jeff's wife Eileen first, propping her up against the bed-head. Jeff they dumped at the foot of the bed, his face poked to the carpet by the sole of a trainer, defeated by the urine seeping down the front of his pyjama bottoms.

And then began a long wait, frustrating for all concerned. Fred prowled with his bat and pushed perpetual cigarettes through his suffocating synthetic face. This was like a boring night in the cells for him. He peered out of the window, sensing that something had to be kicking off somewhere, and feeling like a nine-to-fiver, a straight, a stiff, in his devotion to unavoidable duty.

Barney first filed through the Harcross's record collection, disappointed to discover only *Abba's Greatest Hits* and *The Carpenters' Singles*. He wasn't that bothered about the wait, it was all part of it, Jimmy had taught him that. He enquired aloud, about the possibility of anything by Pulp, Blur or Nirvana, but such was his gnarled pronunciation, according to the police report, that Geoff and Eileen took these few words they could understand to be apocalyptic hints at their eventual fate. He went further in mentioning Massive Attack and Dreadzone. Eventually, it seemed, Barney - who just had to be Ronald - perched on a hard-backed chair and immersed himself in one of Jeff's books on the Second World War, the slit of the rubber quivering as his lips followed the text.

Eight hours is time for a lot of thinking. Too much time really, if you're pressed face down on a carpet with your hands tied behind your back, life flashing by in snatches, a wet crotch and premonitory phrases containing the words 'pulp', 'blur', 'nirvana' 'massive attack' and 'dreadzone' ringing in your brain.

When the time came, the robbery itself was over in a matter of minutes and the small queue of pensioners already gathered outside the post office were able to supply astigmatic details, not including the plate number or make of a blue, or perhaps grey, car in which Fred and Barney sped off.

The story, in simplified form, had been plastered across the front page of the local paper at the time. It turned out that Jeff and Eileen had been weeks away from retirement. They spoke naively of the heartbreak of their belongings being destroyed in front of them, and of thinking they were going to die. The keen young reporter was called Jo Hinchcliffe, and they really opened up to her. On reading such reports, I often tried to imagine what it would feel like standing there and unflinchingly pumping victims for information, and this one seemed to go further than most. The couple provided elaborate detail, which in hard print had the effect of making them seem rather feeble-minded, and the writer somewhat patronising.

The story prompted the usual spate of letters demanding the return of the birch and gallows, but was soon forgotten in the perpetual clamour for new sensation.

Pickles and Raven were arrested in a stolen blue Astra in Leeds two days later. In the car were a number of martial arts weapons, but no bats or masks. There was a large bag of mushrooms in the dash and when searched the two men managed to muster up a handful of E's, temazepam, and four thousand in notes between them. The money could not be traced back to the post office, but that, in any case, would have meant little. They were arrested and held, but it became apparent that nothing of any consequence would stick.

And they were both denying it all of course. They were not in the area at the time of the robbery, and had alibis. Raven was a veteran. The money, they claimed, had come from the sale of expensive musical equipment, in what had been a strictly cash transaction, also involving the stolen car.

Whilst all this hardly cast the duo as conscientious pillars of the community, I was aware there was little that could effectively be used against them. With no positive identifications and a zero from forensic the case would stall, the optimistic charges initially entered - burglary, robbery, assault - would be removed, and the lesser charges whittled down to what would actually stick. Studying the file, it sickened me to realise we were looking at nothing more than car theft, being in possession of a grade A controlled drug, and the usual driving offences.

Handling was a remote outside chance, possession of offensive weapons a possibility. Peanuts. But since Pickles was in breach of a previous suspended, I was prepared for such an eventuality and hopeful he would at least be given the maximum sentence the magistrates could impose. Raven, however, had too long a history for something as trifling as this to make much difference.

There were histories for both Pickles and Raven, the latter's being nothing more than a potted biography, but just as I settled down to study them that evening I was interrupted by a persistent, if rubbery and inoffensive banging on my door.

I opened my sparse, studious and self-contained world to the historian, Mr Gittings, and his wife - Sally's parents - whose impact was gentle, but at the same time instant and all-pervading. They perambulated in, both grinning broadly. They seemed to somehow shoot in all directions at once around my bare rooms, pointing fingers into every nook and cranny and peering quizzically at shadows, before Mr Gittings finally squared up to me, in his mild manner. He has a wild mane of silver hair and a bulbous nose. His clothes are bohemian baggy cord and faded denim. His wife is trim and well-preserved; wears leggings and trainers and no make-up.

'James,' he shook his head with a rueful smile, 'why haven't you called us? We deserve a little bit of consideration, surely, two old codgers in their dotage?'

'Travellers in the autumn of life,' his wife said dreamily.

He turned to her then, in wonderment, pointing towards the window.

'Even the curtains have gone,' he said, as if delivering a punch-line.

Mrs Gittings clucked in what was supposed to be, I imagine, disgust, but managed to sound both playful and concerned.

'Where is she?' she said.

I must say I had plenty of time for the Gittings, especially him. Or used to, before the frontiers changed. When we'd dined with them before things between me and Sal went sour, he was an endless supplier of beguiling anecdotes. On one occasion, I remember, we were looking out from a pub's dining room window and he nodded across the road.

'Used to be a zoo,' he'd said, chewing thoughtfully and squinting benignly across at a slice of waste ground. 'Back in 1844. The Wakefield Zoological Gardens.'

It was the sort of thing he was always coming out with, and the way he looked across at the rubble it was as if he knew every detail of what had once happened there. The zoo, he said on that occasion, had only opened for three weeks before a bear escaped and killed a woman, and it was closed down.

I think at the time I mocked this assertion, in my boorish, wine-mellowed manner, but later I checked and it turned out to be quite true. After that I was in awe of what, with a gentle prompt, he'd reveal about wherever we happened to be, what the Vikings or the Edwardians or whoever had got up to, who built what where, and for what purpose. He reminded me of a tribal wise man telling stories which may have been passed down or dreamt up, or a mixture of the two, it hardly mattered. It was the way he would explain things, as if he were indeed communing with ghosts on our local stomping ground, and the way he always found some focus on the horizon between there and here, with kindly, amused eyes.

The Gittings household, where my wife grew up, was a huge, shambling, chaotically-crammed town house from the centre of which emanated a tranquillity to which I was far from accustomed. Sally and her brother, Alan, my 'best man', would tease and torment each other as if they had yet to leave the play-pen, then fall into slumberous reminiscences, only to emerge from them squabbling and defiant, as the historian and his wife grinned on.

Perhaps if I'd had a brother or sister things would have been different.

But picture me at their family gatherings, stiff and out of place. Generosity, warmth, seemed to me unnecessarily demonstrative. The private symbolism which coursed through their conversations was like some rich golden seam I could only cast a flicker at, before turning away.

'She did, didn't she, Mum?'

Surly Alan, with his rebellious tattoo, was a completely different person in the presence of his parents. He'd been a disappointment to them when younger, but typically, they'd stuck by him, and gradually he'd calmed down.

'No, it was you.'

'Well what about her?'

'She never stopped talking. I don't know what finally shut her up. It wasn't us.'

'Dad? Remember how we used to have to sit in the back of the car, every Sunday morning?'

'Sally would close her eyes,' the historian confirmed, 'with a pin over the map.'

'And I would drive,' Mrs Gittings said, 'wherever it landed. Didn't matter if it took an hour or eight, that was our destination. We made sandwiches, me and Sally. Always. Before we set off. Stop you two grumbling.'

'You always wanted Dad to drive,' Sally told Alan.

'Only because he'd get there quicker.'

'We didn't want to get there. We didn't want to know where we were going.'

'Why?'

'Typical chauvinist conditioning,' Mrs Gittings said.

'Dad wouldn't have done it,' Sally said.

'He'd have stopped at the first pub.'

'We saw everything, but what do we remember?'

'Churches.'

'Cliffs.'

'Petrol stations.'

'Quarries. There was a time when all we stopped at was quarries.'

'Because of the rock formations. Where else would you see them?'

'Where did we go, though?' Alan asked.

'Anywhere and everywhere.'

'Scotland once.'

'I remember that,' Alan said.

'So do I son, so do I.'

'Before the roads were like they are now.'

Listening to this politely, I was a piece of rock, and not a land-locked rock, but a chunk in the middle of a vast sea, so cold and alone and still, the barnacles could settle on my soul.

Christmas, they exchanged stockings full of novelty items. If we stayed home, the Gittings would come around to deliver them. Sally received one from both her mother and father, and from Alan. So did James Junior. I received some kind of composite from everyone, as if I wasn't really expected to join in. The contents of these stockings were rich in personal observation. *I saw you admiring that*, they said, *I watched as you enjoyed this, I know some things will always be your favourite. We love you, no matter what.*

That was the simple message behind the ritual I could never somehow condone. The contents of my stocking said: *What do you want? How can we help?*

Books were heaped in every imaginable place at the Gittings' - under tables and behind sofas, down the sides of armchairs and towering on the top of the cistern in the toilet. The childhood and teenage accumulations of the two children lay in piles around the rooms, awaiting reinvestigation

Johnny Seven guns and rag-dolls, battered *Corgi* cars and racks of board games - *Ker-Plunk*, *Mouse-Trap*, *Twister*. Christmas and birthday cards, dating back a couple of decades, were hung like over-ripe cardboard fruit on strings stretched across the walls. The fronts of wall units were papered with skittish finger paintings, long-yellowed and curled at the edges.

It was a far cry from the ordered estate of James Montgomery Turner, and I deliberately distanced myself from its overbearing warmth.

All that laughter, I concluded, had to be unhealthy.

'James,' Mrs Gittings repeated kindly, 'where is she?'

'Isn't she with you?' I replied. 'I assumed that's why you were here. Salvage and scrap. I think I've a couple of gold fillings we can prise out.'

They looked at me strangely, the grins becoming uncertain.

'We realised things were off-kilter,' the historian said, his voice suddenly a whisper, as if he were receiving advice from beyond, 'but we could have helped.'

'Oh, you helped all right,' I said, 'creeping about in the middle of the night, stripping things bare, uprooting the fixtures and fittings.'

Here again, my words were met with a mutually baffled pair of faces.

'Not us, James,' Mrs Gittings said haughtily, 'We wouldn't come to you unless you wanted us.'

'That lump of a brother of hers, your son, helping himself uninvited to the contents of my fridge.'

Dual inscrutability.

'So is Sally not here?' the historian urged, if indeed he understood the concept of urgency.

My reply, his manner assured me, might take a week, or a decade, or a millennium, it didn't seem to matter.

'Don't you know where she is?'

The conversation was now becoming just as puzzling to me as it seemed to them.

'She brought James to us, but that was a week ago,' Mrs Gittings said. 'Asked us to look after him for a day or two, while she sorted things out with you. We understand things have been hard. Sometimes they are.'

'When was that?'

She visibly counted back through the days.

'Sunday, like I said, late in the evening.'

The same night. After we'd argued over that stupid dog, of course.

'And then you all came here and stripped the place bare as I slept.'

The two grins which reacted to this, were in the negative.

'I think we'd better all sit down,' I said miserably.

Corduroy and lycra obligingly hit patches of carpet where chairs used to be.

Fourteen

An uneasy idea entered my head. As I talked to the historian and his wife this idea, which I had previously had no reason at all to entertain – indeed would have dismissed out of hand – began to cement itself insidiously.

She had another man.

Within minutes it was certainty.

The Gittings, I could tell, were also harbouring this notion and their attitude towards me changed somewhat. They assured me – in a bid to change the unspoken subject – of the well-being of my son, and of their willingness to continue looking after him until things were sorted out.

But did they really want it sorting out? Were they simply hoping for a lack of acrimony in a situation they saw as irredeemable? Could I trust them at all, expect them to even consider my position, let alone act in my interests?

Mrs Gittings, who'd assumed an easy lotus position and was going a little blue around the ankles, took out a packet of photographs there on the carpet. They showed James Junior in his element, given the run of that old house, that shrine-like white elephant stall with its toys and trappings and temptations, each photo having somewhere at its edges a pair of hands, which were outstretched in symbolic welcome to the world of happiness.

'He's a little imp,' Mrs Gittings said.

'Full of mischief,' the historian added. 'He'll be able to talk a glass eye to sleep before long. It's 'mummy' this and 'cat' and 'juice' all the time.'

And then, inexplicably, they both raised their arms in the air as if about to dive into an abyss and chorused, 'Infinity and beyond!'

For some reason they started to giggle rather pathetically.

Mrs Gittings then twirled an invisible revolver from her hip.

'Reach for the sky!' she said in a husky baritone.

'Howdy, partner,' her husband added, a little half-heartedly now.

Perched on the remaining stiff-backed chair I looked down on them there with utter bewilderment.

'*Toy Story,*' she said, jerking a thumb at the historian. 'He can recite it for you verbatim if you want.'

'Must have seen it thirty times over the last week,' he confirmed. 'Marketing phenomenon of the decade. Next year there'll be a shortage of spider babies, you mark my words.'

'Or Mister Potato-heads.'

'Sally's promised him a Buzz Lightyear.'

'Who?'

'Jimmy. For Christmas.'

I had no idea what they were talking about, who Buzz Lightyear was. I was missing out, because my wife had another man. Misery pressed down and enveloped me.

Mentally I scanned an identification parade looking for a likely face, but Mr X remained a shadowy figure, a featureless *Milk Tray* man, an indistinct dashing blade. Though I couldn't see him yet, I could smell him already, a sickening combination of pine forests and car oil, wood shavings and bonfires. I culled stored images from catalogues and car adverts to summon up his blue, square jaw, the curves of the desk in his office, the angle of his bedside lamp, his biceps and hobbies, his power meetings and work-outs, the glint of his watch and the angle of his fist as it connected with the gearstick of my own car.

Had they laughed quietly to each other, as they crept between my house and my car, piling the BMW with treasures? Did their eyes twinkle as they stole away into the night? Did he – Mr X – keep the engine running as Sally deposited James Junior with the Gittings? Did they kiss then, in my car, trembling with relief and anticipation? But surely, I thought, they'd hired a van too? Perhaps he drove that for her and she followed in the car?

The Gittings were probably in on it anyway. Doubtless they approved. I could imagine the sort of advice they would give their only daughter. And her brother too, gritting his teeth with sibling protectiveness. Though I remember little about our wedding, and the events preceding it, I do remember looking around from the dinner table at one point and seeing Sally and that lunk in heated, whispered exchange. She was remonstrating. The veins bulged on his neck. He glanced across at me and his eyes were as effective as a forehead connecting with the bridge of my nose. Pure hatred. The wish to do me intense violence. Why, I have no idea.

How long, I wondered, had it been going on, this approved liaison? Sally was easily capable of keeping secrets from me, that I was well aware of. I envied her ability to keep things to herself, to veil her feelings. I have always thought of myself, with a twinge of shame and regret, as a blurter, a confessor to anyone willing to listen. But then she had people around her, who were concerned and protective, though at the same time once removed, out of the thick of it. All of a sudden I felt like Little Orphan Annie.

The questions and the unsavoury imaginings came thick and fast then, and the identification parade was growing longer by the second, with old schoolfriends, the family doctor, vague shop assistants, Uncle Tom Cobbley and all tagging on to its line. She went to a gym twice a week, doubtless filled with bulging, preening morons in vests. Squash bachelors sipping iced water and clutching their kitbags like security blankets. Iron-pumping estate agents, swim-happy surgeons, step-walking sergeants.

Sally wasn't that upset about the dog, Kevin, at all, it occurred to me, that was just an excuse. She'd brought about our argument on the night in question deliberately, as a means of supplying her with the motivation and the justification for finally leaving me, with the blessing of everyone else who had a stake in her happiness.

Other incidents jostled for attention in my crowded head, all imbued with fresh significance. No more than phrases - the way they were said rather than their actual content - and gestures, all the equivalent of two fingers turned from a victory salute to a cuckold's slap with an easy flick, but so many of them, flooding at me. They quickly combined to give me a completely different picture of Sally and the way she behaved in the weeks prior to her leaving, and to erase any shred of doubt. I'd even begun to imagine there was something wrong with me, that her coldness and her lack of interest in anything I had to say or do was my own fault.

Those bills were another thing, the mystifying purchases itemised in towering banks of figures which surely should have suggested to me that something was going on.

She had been nest-building elsewhere, padding out some cosy cottage with her tasteless tat. Or wining and dining her paramour, showering him with lavish gifts, keeping him amused with the purchase power of our plastic.

How could I have been so blind? What had I imagined Sally was doing all day, anyway? Watching daytime TV, I suppose, cleaning and looking after our son. The fact that I couldn't remember her face on our wedding day, I realised, might suggest a slight lack of attention to her inner life afterwards.

'I'll come and collect James,' I told the Gittings. They exchanged a worried glance. They were in on it, no doubt about that now. My father was right, in the end, not to trust them.

'Well James,' the historian said, smugly, benignly, 'I don't know. We'd need to speak to his mother first, that's the thing. That's really why we came.'

'Knocking, as opposed to breaking and entering,' I suggested.

This was the bottom line: I needed permission now, to see my own son.

Mrs Gittings put her teacup down, untangled her knotted legs and heaved herself up, nodding at the historian. She put a hand on my shoulder.

'Better give it a day or two,' she said. 'I'm sure Sally will be in touch, and there are things you ought to give some thought to, both of you.'

I didn't see them out.

Fifteen

So now I have a visitor. Trevor steers me towards the table at the centre of the room. The tables are white, moulded plastic. Screws flank the frame, oblivious, tooled-up. Some heads turn and primate teeth are bared at my entrance, but mainly the other cons are too busy french-prising bags of smack from the pinched lips of their harassed better halves, muttering at tabloids or squinting at Pools coupons and periodically barking at the runtish kids who dance and squeal in the smoke. And nobody recognises Jo Hinchcliffe. Erect at my side, Trevor stares down any lingering looks.

She gazes up from an affectedly down-market women's magazine to survey me, cool as you like, proud of herself. She's incognito, the look she's contrived for the occasion being Small Town Hair Salon: head scarf and trowelled mascara, baggy jumper, tight jeans and heels. Her television persona would be completely wrong for this place, lacking that put-upon pallor, the plagued tinges and rims, the stylistic splashes of man-made fibre and thin silver. Her health and Riviera glow is mistaken for tubed orange, a Kentucky-fried coating, and the superiority she exudes, for a combination of brassiness and raw nerves.

The television likes her these days, or at least a small pocket of it does, a regional snippet, the kind that still only exists in backwaters. I've watched her, trying to read the autocue without stumbling, as if off-camera some technician is deliberately moving his hand up and down in front of her concealed screen. She is given to colouring as she trips over hastily assembled sentences and to having to halt herself mid-gesture from scratching her hot scalp under its lacquered helmet. The heat of the studio seems to pervade my cell as I watch.

Her programme spotlights the brighter side of local life, with the emphasis on charity and sport: rugby league cheerleading teams, all-night darts throwing competitions, marching kazoo bands and pensioners stitching quilts by candlelight for the local bowls club. It is sandwiched between the weather and the end of the in-depth regional news.

At the tail of it she is obliged to joke with her co-presenter - some chiselled smoothie rescued from the dug-out of minor league football commentary - and the ache in the jaws of the couple as they exchange this excruciating banter has, on occasions, quite touched me. Inevitably, it involves tasting food, which Jo always has to go into raptures over.

'Mmmm,' she groans, eyes heavenwards.

'Well, I don't think I'll touch another pancake/ice cream/chocolate for a year,' he replies, rubbing the shirt under his buttoned blazer as he squares up to the camera.

There is then a brief, inaudible exchange under the theme music, punctuated by the most insincere laughter as the credits roll.

Jo was, after all, nothing more than a cub reporter on a local newspaper the first - and only - time we met. But now she's on television. In other circumstances, if I were her father, for instance, I would be proud of her.

If I was feeling vindictive however, and not so desperate for conversation, I would blame her for a good part of my predicament. The fact that we ended up in bed together counts for nothing now, but despite these conflicts I am somehow pleased to see her.

'You're filling out,' she observes, ice dry. 'Something must be agreeing with you. You got my letter didn't you?'

I nod. 'How's the truth?'

'Elusive,' she comes back, without blinking, 'but I maintain my duty to it.'

'Only it doesn't matter so much now does it?'

'Why?'

'Well, you're on the telly. Out there in Playland.'

'So why doesn't it matter?'

'Come on, I've watched you.'

'Have you? What d'you think?'

'I don't think anything very much, actually. A kind of soothing numbness comes over me when you're speaking. My mind empties. I forget I ever even had thoughts. So you must be doing your job.'

She makes as if to slap my wrist, a pleasant, tactile gesture. We're flirting, of course, in our fashion, the way we did that first and only time, after the Pickles and Raven trial. She laughs and lights a cigarette, a long menthol thing with several gold bands at its filter. The wrong cigarette, of course, light years from the mean roll-up which passes for currency in here. It betrays her disguise, and if she's not careful they'll start to notice.

'Why don't you sit down?' she says.

'I don't know why you're here, I don't think there's anything worth pursuing really.' I sit down anyway. 'Well perhaps I do, but I don't see why I should help.'

Trevor pats me on the shoulder as if I've just been eased into a dentist's chair.

'Don't you have a little suit with arrows on it?'

'Only when I'm breaking rocks.'

'It's not how I imagined it at all, this.'

'That's obvious. You look like you're dressed up for a film.'

'I thought they'd have grills, or reinforced glass between us.'

I'm in subdued pinstripe to wind them up, an open-necked collar my only concession.

'No,' I reply.

'You could just jump up and strangle me or something.'

'Yes.'

'Look, this idea I've got,' she says. 'What d'you think? I want you to take it seriously, because it could happen.'

'Don't you think I take you seriously? I had to take what you wrote seriously enough.'

'Forget about that now.'

'It's a little difficult in here, but anyway, I'm not sure I can take your show seriously.'

'Why not?'

'I hope the salary's sufficient.'

'It's what people want, what they expect.'

'Cosy.'

'So?'

'You're spoon-feeding them crap.'

Jo scowls.

'I'm aware of its limitations, the point is, there's potential there. Okay, I know it's not earth shattering. We don't have the budget, for one thing. But my producer knows that too. She says we're a strong team. Synergetic. And she's up for something a bit more hard-hitting.'

'So?'

'So, that's why we want to take a chance on you.'

'How are you taking a chance? I suppose I'm about as big a celebrity as you can muster, is that it?'

'If we can arrange it, would you do it? All you'd have to do is ask some of your fellow inmates hard-hitting questions. They'd volunteer. Jump like a shot at the opportunity of getting their stories across. And you could tear them apart, like you would do if you were still in court. Only, of course you'd be a criminal too.'

'I haven't done anything, though.'

'The prison authorities must want the publicity. They'd let us film it here, I'm certain. Maybe even from your cell or something. No, that wouldn't work, would it? We'd need to mock up some kind of courtroom. *Kangaroo Court*, what about that for a title?'

'I haven't done anything.'

'Nobody says you have, but it would give people something to think about, wouldn't it? It might do your case some good.'

'How? Everybody thinks I'm guilty anyway. I'm in prison, for God's sake. Not just for a crime I didn't commit, but for one they haven't even found a name for.'

'Try fraud.'

'I'm innocent.'

'Until proven guilty.'

'And I don't see how making a fool of myself on television would help matters.'

'It would if you get off. Even if you don't. The fact that you're someone with a high sense of his own superiority is enough. They'd have to question what you were about.'

'Why?'

'Because you're in prison. In any case, I think the consensus is beginning to swing in your favour, crime's back and big at the moment. Its fighters are being feted. It's been long enough now for most of them to have forgotten just how obnoxious you were.'

'You haven't a clue what it's like. Not being able to move about freely. Having the lights switched off for you when you don't want to sleep.'

'Well when they dip the switch, I want you to think grooming. If you can do that for me. Just the usual things.'

'I think about other things, now. Pornography, violence. The smell's in the back of my throat.'

'Consider your rough edges, blunted, smoothed. Try and see this as a period of transition, that's all.'

'Fuck off.'

'Think a future beyond the end of your nose, James. Six months from now, consider what you'll look like, how you'll sound. Where you might be.'

'I don't know anything about it. I want to tell them what they want to hear. How Liz Armstrong ran off with my money. Where she took it.'

She shrugs.

'Why don't you tell them?'

'Obviously because I don't know.'

'The prisons are full of them. Sob story merchants.'

'You only found out what a prison was like two minutes ago.'

'It's enough.'

'I want them to catch up with her.'

'They won't waste too much time. They've got you.'

'You know I'm innocent.'

I watch the amber tip of her cigarette snake its way through white ashes to the gold bands.

'I don't feel responsible in any way for what happened to you.'

'I was a fool.'

'Perhaps so, but your career's over with the CPS, so when you do get out you'll have to think about something else.'

'I'm hardly enamoured with the media.'

This also makes her laugh, a gin-cracked gurgle which sends premature crow's feet scattering around the precise lines of her waterproof mascara. I find myself wondering what underwear she has on. This is what it makes you do, talking to Trevor, listening to the rest of them.

'Don't make me feel so shameless, Mister Turner,' she looks down, then back at me slyly, somehow confirming her upwardly-mobile underwear status, 'you're not so stoic. I know if I can get this project off the ground you won't be able to resist. You're a sound-bite natural, you look the part and there's enough of a story by now.' She scowls impatiently. 'What do you expect me to do, chain myself to railings until they let you out? I would if I could, honest Indian. Help me, though. Think grooming. Think image. Think projection.'

'Do you know what they call me in here,' I say, 'the West Indians? The Righteous Brother.'

Jo Hinchcliffe gives me an appreciative and appraising slow nod.

'That's good,' she says, 'isn't it? Don't you think that's good enough? It's a start. They were an old Tamla Motown group, weren't they, like the Four Tops?'

'They were white.'

'Can I take that back to her? We could even call it *The Righteous Brother*, perhaps, or *The Righteous Brother's Kangaroo Court*, and you can rant and rave like you used to do in court, when you had everything on your side.'

With that she pecks me on the cheek. Generously, it seems, or perhaps the physical contact is just so unexpected.

As I watch her weave her way through the clusters to the exit I try and imagine the television slot she has in mind. James Hartley Turner sweating under a layer of cosmetics, eyes bulging and fingers flashing accusations. The larger-than-life version of myself I pictured representing my mother at my father's imaginary trial. Cowed opposition, unflinching camera angles.

And then it would cut back to Jo and her partner on the couch.

'Mmm...' she'd say, 'food for thought there...and speaking of food, let's see how they're getting on in the kitchen...' Chiselled-cheeks would rub his stomach.

How could it possibly be anything other than trite?

But there would be hospitality, banquets and opening nights, celebrity galas, chauffeured cars, pretty young media women... Could I let her take me by the hand and lead me into Playland?

Trevor pats me on the shoulder.

'Ready?' he asks, as if I'm a debutante about to be escorted down her first ballroom staircase.

Sixteen

Your first fumbled sex, remember that? Lips that go all the way around the houses. The moons of your fingertips on cold straps and intricate eyelets. Thumbs down folds.

It is with a girl with shoulder-length hair which smells of apples outside the ultra-violetly lit Mecca ballroom, with its mock-velvet booths and the palm-fronded upstairs bar, embellished with Zulu spears and shields. Demolished, years ago.

She wears ankle socks over black tights and clumpy crepe heels. The stars shine down. You kiss her, or she kisses you, it's hard to say. Her mouth tastes of spearmint. After it is over, which will be much too soon, you'll have to figure out a way to get back into the school dormitory, but your arm creeps up inside her leather coat and traces the shape of her wire-strengthened bra underneath her thin blouse. She wears a necklace with the letters of her name on it, but this is not sufficient to imprint what she was called in your mind. You wrestle with zippers and buttons, not feeling the cold night air, and finally comes the shock of what it actually feels like, inside.

You never spoke a word to her. It wasn't done.

Half a dozen girls like her were in the courtroom that morning, chewing the veneer from their lips as they awaited the outcome. Brash and mawkish girls with long, straight hair and pale complexions, in cut-off track suits and chokers.

Ronald Pickles, the mugger, stared at me once again from the dock. I imagined those eyes peering through the slits in a synthetic mask in the likeness of Barney Rubble. A blank, shocked, quizzical expression, conveyed by a pursed exclamation of a mouth, a smooth blaze of yellow hair.

At his side was Raven, with his blunt features and knocked-about nose, a nose which looked as if it had been used as a doorstop for a decade or so. A nose that was always destined for perpetually pecking at concrete. I'd stood avoiding the eyes of Jimmy Raven in that spot at least half a dozen times before.

The guilt of that pair was inherent in the way they stood, the way they smirked and exchanged conspiratorial whispers, flanked between the two Group Four security guards. The girls smiled and waved at them. A couple ran up to the dock bearing gifts and were shooed back by the usher.

I had imagined our eye contact at this moment, the shock and disbelief of the mugger Pickles at seeing me behind his fat file, and the satisfaction I would gain from this.

In the few days since opening that file, however, something had changed inside me, and any feeling of a hunger being sated was lost on my sick, empty stomach.

Phone calls to everyone I could think of had failed to locate Sally. Nor had Liz Armstrong deigned to contact me. My imagination became a grim torturer, parading gruesome pictures of deceit before my eyes and jabbing me with tiny details like insistent barbs at my heart.

It must have been going on, I decided, almost since James Junior was born.

I saw it as a considered move on Sally's part, one arrived at as I clutched her hand at the side of the hospital bed and she screamed and writhed and cursed like the mill women, as the latest addition to the Turner line, in keeping with our stubborn streak, did his utmost to stay put.

The birth of my son had not been easy for either of us, but Sally was at a distinct advantage, being drugged to the eyeballs. I had wanted to be there for her, and for the child, of course, but the cosy notion of myself as a useful member of that fiercely self-contained, antiseptic female community, with their starched uniforms, scrubbed skin and steely implements, and all that compulsive hand-washing, soon wilted under the harsh fluorescence of the birthing suite's stark lights.

In pregnancy Sally gained not only the single-minded purpose associated with her condition, sticking rigidly to diet charts and exercise programmes, but also a sexiness which hinged on her sense of power. She certainly seemed to laugh more in those months, and we were never as close. We made simple mobiles, and bought enough Disney wallpaper to animate a full-length film. I resigned myself to smoking my very occasional fat Cuban cheroot out on the doorstep and making weekend visits to Tots R Us. The credit card statements started becoming so lengthy I began to ignore them.

It was to be a natural birth, and one during which she'd actively conduct the celestial trumpets and heavenly choirs an American hypnotist had convinced her would strike up.

But once the pangs started in the birthing room, it was a matter of mere minutes before depravity, if not madness, set in. The oxygen and air was of little use (to either of us), and after two shots of pethidine had limped around her system I began to despair of meekly holding her vice-like hand and uttering hopeless platitudes of false comfort. A succession of wasp-waisted and scraped-skull dragons brushed me aside to stab an available vein and cast a cursory glance at the blood, bone and sinew between the stirrups. I was invited to examine the admirable dilation, since they like to get men involved. This I politely declined. Eventually Sally sat bolt upright and, face contorted to the extent that I honestly believed her head would begin to rotate, spewed out the longest line of expletives available to her.

It was at that point I realised I should leave. James eventually poked his rascally little head out twelve hours later, delivered by Caesarean section. Sally, thankfully, slept through it. Blurry-eyed, I watched Mike Tyson swiftly pummel Frank Bruno into a pantomime pulp on cable TV in some all-night drinking den nearby, then staggered home for perhaps the most dreamless and uninterrupted sleep I've ever had.

At some time during all that, she decided she wanted someone else. I don't know how I knew this, but I did. The smell of him was getting keener: his aftershave, his car interior.

Afterwards, once the excitement had died down, she gained access, via James Junior, to a whole new social world of surgeries and baby groups. And she started going to that gym in an attempt to recover her figure. In the few days preceding the Pickles and Raven trial I phoned around all the places I could think of in my attempts to track her down, and found other faces for Mr X - health visitors and baby-group leaders, nurses and relaxation-class helpers, devoted fathers, all of them bearded, and to my mind dubiously motivated.

The night before the trial, there had also been something of a misunderstanding at the residence of Mr and Mrs Gittings.

I had wanted James Junior back, but given the fraught and somewhat worse-for-wear state in which I arrived to claim him, they were reluctant to hand him over.

Much as I liked the couple, I could not accept their interference at that precise, swooping and semi-coherent moment in time. Reason was not something I wanted to listen to. It shames me to say that when the kindly old historian attempted to block my access, I must have pushed him aside rather more forcibly then I intended.

Stumbling with deceptive swiftness up the stairs, oblivious to the commotion in my wake, and pausing only to aim an ineffectual karate chop at Sally's childhood dolls house at the top of the stairs, I crashed into my wife's former bedroom, where I instinctively knew James would be. He was nestled in flowery padding and quilting, framed by lace and fringes. He had a cartoon-size copy of *The Wizard of Oz* in his arms, and it only took the removal of this to bring about the most agitated blue fit on an infant's part it has ever been my misfortune to witness. Perhaps I panicked and he sensed my fear, but whatever, he writhed and resonated like an electric eel as I pulled him up to me, bellowing all the while, so that I stumbled back against a pile of books which were towering on a bedside table, bringing the lot down on top of my wriggling, hysterical son and myself. Bending to his will, I released him, finding it hard enough to get back to my feet on my own. I don't know if I passed out briefly then, but the next thing I saw was James in the cautious arms of Mrs Gittings, from whose lips was spilling a melodic litany of comfort, while the historian steered me gently by the arm towards the door. Neither of them was grinning, I noticed, and he had the most severe looking purple gash trailing from his temple around his left eye to his cheek.

'This really doesn't make any sense, you know. Better go, old chap,' he said. 'I do hope you can sort all this out.'

How I came to be in my own bed the following morning, possessed of a startling clarity, is beyond me now.

The Gittings had become tarred with the same brush as their daughter in my doubtless troubled mind. Wasn't it all part of some conspiracy, an attempt to scatter the Turner ranks? To tether James Junior to their tender concern, to indoctrinate him and wilfully weaken me, to sow the seeds of suspicion and doubt within both of us, to crop the hair of a line of Samsons?

Seventeen

Christmas Day was exactly a week away. It had crept up on me stealthily, preoccupied as I was. Shop windows groaned with garish produce and TV programmes got shorter as the slices of unit-shifting they were sandwiched between became hideously engorged. All major roads were unpassable and an atmosphere of suppressed hysteria descended like syrup, manifesting itself in the glazed looks and the bag-lady appearance of the jovial shoppers who clogged up the precincts.

James Junior, it seemed, would be participating in the festivities over at his grandparents'. The certainty of the family being reunited for the occasion hadn't escaped me.

Neither had the fact that my own invitation would inevitably be delayed in the post.

The advent of festive spirit, however, turned out to be fortunate for Pickles and Raven. There was an air of impatience from the bench, their minds already on last-minute sorties around the toy shops and self-satisfied afternoons of sherry and *The Sound of Music*.

Perhaps if I'd had the joy of observing James Junior's eyes widen in response to a bulging sack of toys at four in the morning to look forward to, the idea of Christmas wouldn't have made me feel so nauseous. Apples and oranges and chocolate selection boxes tumbling onto crisp white sheets, paper shredded and tossed to the carpet.

Outside the court, council workmen were threading a string of plastic bulbs from the courthouse roof to a lamp post across the street. A number of police officers huddled, hopeful of a decent result. They always chose to stay outside until proceedings commenced, I'd noticed. As if they were guilty of something. Some were there to give evidence about the aftermath of the post office robbery and wouldn't be called, others to outline the reasons for the subsequent arrest, and to corroborate the interview tapes. They were not optimistic.

Had he been given the chance, PC John Thewlis would have told the court about the time his ear lobe had almost been bitten off when attempting to arrest Jimmy Raven.

Some police officers were alleged to have been present and to have laid bets at an arranged fight between Raven and a trained albino Doberman, which took place on a farm outside Wakefield one dusky summer's night. The Blue Crooner was down on his luck at that time, according to this legend, club bookings having dried up. The policemen concerned collected their winnings too, the story goes, from the estate trolls who descended in a battered procession of Cortinas and transits, to convey their support and appreciation of the mythical, genetically-engineered racist canine. Raven minced it, they say. If it's true, put the discreet police presence down to strain of the job and the necessary letting off of steam.

PC Angela Roberts, in any case, could have described how the Crooner's apprentice, Pickles, had tried to headbutt her. But those were other crimes of course, and they counted for nothing. The officers complained of their frustration at having to deal with the same faces again and again. Pickles more than Raven these days, apparently. His sheer indifference mocked everything they stood for.

One of them informed me he'd broken into a former girlfriend's flat just two days after the post office robbery. She knew it was him, but wouldn't testify against him. She was having to buy her things back from him now. Stick by sad stick.

The charges of robbery and any attempt to connect the pair to the post office had, as expected, been dropped. This was a salvage and scrap situation. They were pleading guilty to the theft of a car and possession of a controlled drug. The offensive weapons charge was dropped at this point.

Besuited and scrubbed, the duo's shameful cocked snook of sobriety looked even more sinister to me. It was mockery of the highest order and something the magistrates would surely see through, regardless of the fact their minds were doubtless three parts tinsel and snow.

That Pickles and Raven had even attempted a sham stab at decency, with a couple of catalogue discount suits and buckets of aftershave, only compounded their guilt to my way of thinking.

Despite this, I kept my case outline brief and to the point, relying on an arched eyebrow here, a dismissive gesture there, the stress in my voice at certain points giving a clear indication of what should have been obvious but could not be said. The magistrates were required to make a simple equation, nothing more. My description of the outrageous way in which the elderly postmaster and his wife had been terrorised was clipped, and, I fancied, all the more chilling for that. I got away with mentioning it only because the pair had been arrested on suspicion of involvement in the first place, but I managed to get in the fact that they were in a car stolen before the burglary, despite nobody being able to identify it at the scene, and that the physical description of the two masked men seemed something of a coincidence. I then squeezed as much as I could from the stolen car, the drugs and the large amount of money they had on them, and the weapons.

Pickles shook his head with a laughable expression of hurt and outrage at even the mildest accusation. When I attempted to précis his appalling record, simplifying to the extent that I was doing him a favour, Raven simply attempted to drill through to my soul with his eyes. But when I stood down, I was brimming over with blind confidence.

Then, as I slumped onto the bench, the hangover which had been held at bay all morning by a combination of adrenaline and concentration emerged victorious. Bile was in my mouth, bringing back with it little unpleasant snatches of what I'd done and said over at chez Gittings the night before. My nostrils became blocked and I took out a handkerchief and blew, feeling as if a particularly diseased part of my brain was trying to squeeze its way down the capillaries of my nose. I blew again, lurched for the bottle of water and discovered my hands were shaking. The clerk glanced at me with concern.

The defending solicitor was, inevitably, my old adversary Colin Chatterton, that charlatan, decked out in a buffoonish costume:

canary yellow jacket and what looked like tartan plus-fours. We had declined to exchange even cursory nods from our respective corners up to that point.

Now, however, he sidled across to me and put a concerned hand on my arm.

'Are you okay?'

I shook his arm away weakly and managed at the same time to send a ream of papers flapping into the aisle with my other elbow. With a grunt I ducked and scooped them up.

'Fine,' I managed to gasp, climbing back onto my seat and straightening the papers. The courtroom had become insufferably hot and I covertly attempted to loosen my tie. 'Your jacket's giving me a migraine, that's all.'

'Hey, don't take it all too seriously, okay?' He gave me a playful cuff on the shoulder. My stomach felt like some kind of swelling and contracting worm, blocking my lungs one second and taut and empty the next. I kept seeing the gentle historian's face, with the gash down it, heard myself screaming wild accusations I had chosen to block out. I'd certainly used words which had never before been heard in that house.

'I've got this one, you realise that don't you?' Chatterton was whispering, his face looming close. 'No way they're going to buy all that. Sorry, but that's the nature of the beast. You sure you're okay?'

I saw my son - only two years old - sleepily trying to make sense of his drunken father's presence, and then crying for his mother as he was dragged from his bed, pulled down to the carpet as the books thudded and thumped around his ears.

'Get some air at least,' Chatterton said. With that, he shuffled back grinning. As he began his submission, full of cosy adverbs and Enid Blyton similes, I could tell the magistrates were becoming restless. Chatterton's defences were always slow, and I'm surprised more of the criminal fraternity didn't connect his ponderousness to the outlandish sentences they sometimes received. He was an old hippy of the first order in his clownish clothes, with a ring in his ear and a self-conscious goatee. Most of the time he could be found in the corridor smoking and listening with sleepy-eyed solemnity to hyperbolic tales of wrong-place, wrong-time.

Pickles was a young man with certain personal problems he was struggling to overcome, the magistrates were told. How many times had they heard such balderdash? But he was good-hearted and generous to friends and strangers alike. He'd recently developed a keen interest in art and was hopeful of a college placing, the defence line continued, and I wouldn't have been at all surprised to hear of a sudden fondness for animals and small children. He'd voluntarily visited a detoxification unit and was reunited with his former girlfriend. My snort of contempt was clearly audible at that point, earning me an affectionate glance of admonishment from the clerk.

Enid Blyton gave way to mythology as Pickles became first Prometheus already bound to the rock, and then Dionysius, with the sword of Damocles suspended by that single horsehair thread above him. That was when I became certain my learned friend had really lost it. Trying to batter the bench into submission was unwise on the very last sitting before Christmas. But he'd hardly started.

Jimmy Raven's personality was another matter entirely, he asserted. A famous man locally, and a complex man.

'Physical, with a reputation for violence,' Chatterton said, 'but without doubt hampered by his fame.'

I was going to be sick, thin liquid bubbling at the corners of my mouth.

'For where can he go, without his considerable presence being felt, without being recognised by police officers and criminals alike? Jimmy Raven has always been his own man, with one foot outside conventional society, but ask yourself this, *why is he so well-liked*? What is it about him, that draws people, inspires them? Perhaps then, Jimmy Raven is a symbol, the rough diamond we...'

Chatterton's voice became like a mantra. I closed my eyes and put my thumbs to my temples, but the room started to lurch and his words were distant one second, and pressed to my ear the next.

I forced myself to open my eyes again and the sunlight from a side window impacted with a sudden, frightening intensity.

Chatterton was now endlessly circling, regurgitating a few tired phrases and improbable comparisons. The car had been stolen on a whim, to take the two to a party in Leeds, where witnesses would place them on the night of the post office robbery. It was very foolish, they now realised.

Suddenly I was climbing to my feet and using the scrolled posts of the benches like mountaineers' grips to stumble out, uttering profuse apologies over my shoulder, oblivious to the consternation in my wake.

In the toilet I pressed my forehead against the cold tiles and pushed a hand down my throat. The worm in my stomach hissed and spat. I saw the historian's face again. Mrs Gittings comforting my son. Thin yellow fluid pushed from my insides, coaxing the worm out. I sat on the pot. No collage of happy family occasions here, instead a piece of thick black graffiti: *Bom all therd world cuntries now.*

I splashed water on my face in the sink. Spat. Splashed again. Somebody entered, peed self-consciously and left again without comment. My bones ached now, legs tenderised. The mirror had been smashed long ago, its black frame studded over the basin. It reflected enough of my eyes to convey their aqueous, lizard quality. I splashed more water, massaged it into my scalp and neck and forced myself out. At the back of the courtroom a cluster of young girls were obliged to make space for me, whispering and glancing.

Chatterton was still going strong. I sagged there, and finally he ground to a halt and the magistrates retired.

As it happened, they took far less time than usual in reaching a decision and returning. They are wont to give the impression of prolonged backroom debate, the teasing out of truth from each precedent, the frenzied poring over weighty tomes, when the reality is tea and small talk, with the occasional doze and sometimes the quick toss of a coin thrown in. On this occasion though, they were prompt. As the buzzer sounded I resumed my place at the front of the court and looked over at Ronald Pickles in the dock. As he caught my gaze I thought for a moment that he was about to drop his guard, betray the civilised front and reveal himself for the animal he was becoming, but he regained his composure and looked away.

Community Service, Pickles was told, would be a way in which he could prove himself, be of use to society and live up to his stated intention of getting cured and back on the road to the palace of wisdom. In the light of possible victimisation because of who he was, all charges against Raven were dropped.

I knew at that moment that there was no hope.

There were cheers from the duo's addled friends and as I left one of the girls I'd briefly sat next to approached me. Fourteen or fifteen, with a perfect complexion, her cutaway skinny-rib and hipsters emphasising her slenderness, she dashed a lick of hair from her cheek and looked up at me angrily.

'I knew all that stuff you said about my dad and Ronnie was crap,' she said. 'He's not like that at all. Why does everybody pick on him?'

I thought about the first things. Surely there could be no more now?

Outside there was much back-slapping and hand shaking. Pickles and Raven, not to mention Colin Chatterton, were being treated like pop stars or football heroes. There was also much whispering between the males and glances in my direction. I knew what they were saying. I suppose I was staring at them, and returning hard stares. The girls were wide-eyed with admiration, that's the only way I can describe it.

I knew where they would go next. They would all happily descend on the pub which was their territory, to celebrate their victory. The police had already left. None of them had said a word to me. The implication was that I was to blame.

It was then that a cub reporter with sooty eyes and spiky hair appeared at my side. I'd noticed her a few times scribbling earnestly at the press bench. Jo Hinchcliffe told me she'd covered the original story, which I said I'd read, and marvelled at. Then she remarked that I looked disappointed, not to say unwell. There were just the two of us left now, on the court steps. Somewhere around the corner a Salvation Army choir was singing carols and half-heartedly rattling tambourines. It should have been snowing, since it seemed there was so much good will in the air, so much joyeux noel and peace on earth and mercy mild, but the day had barely bothered to break at all and a nibbled, gibbous moon still hung above the court house.

My head ached, the worm in my stomach was still unsettled, but not as ferocious in its writhing. I felt undeniably shabby, but a certain logic seemed to be returning from somewhere.

What was needed, I said, among other things that just seemed to all tumble out, was extermination gangs.

Eighteen

Extermination gangs, I continued, a secret police controlled by the Masons, and if not an actual programme of sterilisation, or better still, extreme and irreversible genetic modification at embryo stage, then forced, annual IQ tests for those without sufficient means who were intending to have children.

'But who's going to have the time to do all that,' she laughed, 'and more to the point, who's going to want to? You're full of bitterness, you know that?'

'I'm bloody terrified. Somebody's got to grasp the nettle.'

'You should calm down or you'll have a coronary or something. Probably within the next five minutes.'

The feigned curiosity and concern my new confidante was doubtless taught in media relations class wilted somewhat when she realised I was steering her towards The Wool Scourer, at the side of the market, in preference to The Barrister's Arms where the colleagues in both our chosen professions were now doubtless happily ensconced.

All eyes - beady, hateful, bloodhound, bloodshot, yellow or glass - turned to look at us as we entered, and then there was a spontaneous, if brief and derisory cheer. Unperturbed, I continued to warm to my theme of radical social reform, waving a crisp twenty pound note in the direction of the sullen, tattoo-doused barman, as Jo Hinchcliffe flushed slightly at the gum-mottled carpet. 'Merry Xmas' was sprayed in silly-string across a mirror, dappled with the encrusted tops of exotic liqueur bottles, at the back of the bar.

'Legalise heroin,' - I was in full flow now - 'in fact give it away on the state in preference to contraceptives and food subsistence cheques. You don't need that nurture. If it doesn't prove an adequate means of birth control I don't know what will.'

I barked all this deliberately into the neck of some elephantine saloon potato garlanded with tinsel. Jo tugged at my sleeve then, and stared at me intently.

'Let's sit down at least,' she said, 'or we're not going to last five minutes.'

'Shall we join them?' I said, making an elaborate show of pointing directly at Pickles and Raven and their entourage. The girls were becoming quite moist at my presence and the potential for excitement it held, but Jo took my arm as if I were the nervous father at her wedding, commanding me to a booth separated from them by a pool table and a frame of slatted panelling.

'Do you take all your cases so personally?' she asked. Her voice was no more than a whisper. She was finally sitting opposite me so that I could observe how pretty she was for the first time. There was the trace of a smile on her lips which suggested she liked taking chances.

'Everything's pretty personal at the moment,' I replied, 'or so it seems.'

'Colin Chatterton isn't like this after a case,' she said.

'He's a smug asshole, that's why.' I glanced over at the crowd, half expecting to see Chatterton there, but of course he was wise enough to keep a professional distance. 'All that false camaraderie and concern really gets on my tits.'

'He seems pretty genuine to me.'

'It's the patronising behaviour of the worst kind of liberal,' I insisted. 'Pretending to have this empathy when he earns more an hour than they draw a fortnight. More than they get for their car radios and dope in a day's dishonest graft.'

'No, he actually cares.'

'Cares about his bank balance, cares about cashing the cheques and keeping them at the other end of a profitable barge pole. Celebrating, is he? Where is he then? Probably preparing his bill for the Legal Aid Board.'

'It must be difficult for him,' she said. 'Think about it.'

I drank a mouthful of whisky which had an instant levelling effect, but again brought back to me the image of the gentle historian, Sally's father, and that gruesome gash on his face. If anything, I had forced too much of the immediate present on him, precariously placed as he was between here and somewhere else.

That much was clear from his resigned tone as he'd led me away from my caterwauling son.

Two grinning crones dressed in skimpy Santa Claus outfits skipped up to us on fishnet-secured slabs of cellulite, jingling a bucket full of loose change under my nose. Before I could say a word Jo Hinchcliffe dipped into her bag and aloofly threw in some scattershot. They giggled away in a waft of pavement hawker eau-de-toilette.

'I suppose your wife's left you then,' she said, lighting a cigarette in a pose that emanated from 1940s Hollywood films - the over-lipsticked, world-weary gangster's moll.

'Certainly has,' I said, raising my glass, 'but you don't want to hear about that, and I certainly bloody don't.'

From the start, Jo Hinchcliffe made me feel like I was in a film, as if all my lines were scripted. At the same time I resented her composure. I could feel that syrupy Christmas thickness in the air again, all mingled with the ache of testosterone. You could cut it with a Stanley knife.

'Do you know them?' I said, deliberately pointing over at Pickles and Raven again. She took hold of my finger and pulled it back to my glass, patting my hand like a sandcastle.

'You'd better stop or I'm going,' she warned.

'Okay, okay,' I said.

But out of the corner of my eye I saw both Pickles and Raven rising. Their movements suggested something deliberate, premeditated.

The girls, Raven's pretty young daughter amongst them, were watching with anticipation from across the room.

'Tell me about yourself then,' I said. But she was watching my friends move to the pool table now. Raven picked up a cue and Pickles, consciously ignoring me, pushed the slot to send the balls crashing to the hole. He then took an age meticulously arranging the yellows and reds in the triangle, before moving the layer of felt from under them.

Jo started to tell me about her work, about being cut adrift in long-dead pit villages until she came up with sufficient column inches: giant marrow competitions and minor roadworks, plucky pensioners and big-hearted dinner ladies...

In the game that was unfolding in front of us, Pickles was revealing himself to be no slouch, taking three of his yellow balls in as many shots and pinning the white behind the cluster that remained for Raven to take his chances.

'Sign of a misspent youth,' I said loudly. Raven was erect at the table for his shot, holding the queue at crotch level, and visibly stiffened further in reaction to my comment. Jo was not oblivious to the atmosphere - far from it - but carried on listing her routine conquests: parish council problems with footpaths, road signs and drains, incensed shopkeepers, terrified tenants, furious ratepayers, bewildered onlookers, horrified neighbours, and a hospital vigil over a young child with a conker stuck up his nose: *It's Nose Blooming Joke!*

She hated Wakefield she said, it was so small-minded and parochial.

'What I do would create a bad impression of anywhere. You walk down the street and all you recognise are the low lifes or the pompous officials. When you over-write the smallest of events, anything that happens is likely to be a disappointment.'

She was simply paying her dues, learning the ropes, until she could find a way in, get a name for herself... At twenty years of age she was already well past the thrill of a number of journalistic firsts - the front-page lead, the by-line and the suburban scoop. And probably others too. She was hungry for more, she said, and determined enough to get it.

Ronald Pickles was making mincemeat of his more experienced mate, outmanoeuvring him at every turn, putting his own balls down and leaving nothing to be retrieved. Raven blustered and stabbed, threatening to push felt through to slate. Then there was nothing left but for Ronald to down the black in a sea of red balls. Heads had turned as the game progressed, and eyes were now full of admiration for his command of the table, the meticulous method of his moves. His way was quite clear, despite Raven's botched attempts to contrive his own snookering situations.

And that's when I lurched to my feet and simply tipped the black ball across the table into a pocket.

There were a few mutters of objection from the people watching, but initially Pickles and Raven just stared at me.

I don't recall what I said exactly, but I started shouting at them, while Jo Hinchcliffe tried to pull me away.

More restraining arms were on my shoulders then, but I can't think for the life of me what I intended to do. Just putting myself in the frame was sufficient. Raven was up close to my face in the melee. Out of the corner of my eye I saw Pickles turning to the girls away from me and spreading his arms out wide, a gesture of comic exasperation. Somewhere in the pub a glass smashed, but it could have been an accident.

'What do you want, you silly wanker?' Raven said. 'Jesus you're stupid. How did it feel, that? Thinking you had it all going your way? Well you don't know fuck all about shit, that's all I'm saying.'

I lunged at him then, with a clenched fist swaying, but he just stepped back, grinning, and there was half the pub hanging onto me, bundling me to the door.

Nineteen

This is how wide of the mark I was: I actually thought Jo Hinchcliffe liked me. She allowed her arm to be taken easily enough, once I'd caught my breath after running from The Wool Scourer, and she climbed into the taxi without questioning our destination, as if it were inevitable. On the journey, as I recall it anyway, she outlined her reasons for detesting the Crown Prosecution Service. It was, she said, a channel for the bigotry and small-mindedness of the comfortable middle classes, or something to that effect. We existed merely as a cipher for police prejudices and as the stool-pigeon of the magistrates, who were nothing more than trumped up Lords of the Manor with a penchant for the admonishment and humiliation of those less fortunate than themselves. She went one step further by reiterating her admiration for that twat Colin Chatterton, describing him as 'in touch with himself' and 'sticking to his principles', or some such nonsense, before spouting that tired cliché of it being far more honourable to have protected one innocent person from injustice, than to have meted out punishment to a thousand. I was ready to hurl her from the taxi at that point.

And then she reminded me of a particular incident, the details of which I didn't remember at all. It had made a lasting impression on her, however, in one of her first court sittings apparently. It was not a remarkable case, merely concerning a couple of the sorry individuals from the tedious non-payment-of-fines lists which were generally brain stormed in the ten minutes before lunch, for fear of clogging up the court's time with mumbled excuses and mute flushes.

This particular couple, Jo Hinchcliffe claimed, were not in court due to fines incurred on their own account, but to answer for those of troublesome offspring. She was fat and flushed and penitent as a nun, in crimplene and flip-flops; he had the peeled countenance of an unchoosy hard drinker. When asked why they had not paid these fines, he had grinned idiotically and she had answered that they had other commitments, which apparently amounted to no more than gargantuan food bills for their tentacle-like tribe, and a hire purchase agreement on a TV. At which point, I was supposed to have rounded on her and asked why, once her offspring had found the weight of the law around their ears and obliged her to make sacrifices for their inadequate upbringing, she hadn't immediately returned the television set?

'You spoke to her like a child, with her useless husband gaping on and grinning at you.' Jo Hinchcliffe said. 'Not even that, you scolded her like an animal. You were enjoying her misery, her total uselessness, and your power. You would have gone further, with the slightest encouragement, like any Nazi.'

I started to protest at that point, but she talked me down.

'You didn't even think she deserved a television set,' she said, shaking her head in wonderment. 'Not even worth a fucking television set, in this day and age, despite all she was coping with. I wanted to cry for her, I really did. To think anybody wasn't even worth that. That pitiful husband of hers should have climbed down from the dock and thumped you. I've seen you do it to other people too.'

Seemingly in response to her tone, the Asian taxi driver threw me a macho and uncomprehending dagger through his rear-view mirror.

'You have a lot to learn, my dear,' I said.

'Nothing you lot can teach me.'

'Well what did they spend their money on?' I asked her. 'How much d'you think it costs to get a face as permanently raw and sandblasted as that?'

'I think you'd like things the way they were back in the middle ages,' she continued, 'with a collection of men like yourself lording it over villages full of underfed and ignorant peasants.'

'Sounds workable.'

I must confess I couldn't remember the couple she was referring to and it saddened me, this lack of respect for my work, which I saw as being closer to her own than she could perhaps have imagined. I had more than a grudging regard for the media.

It was, as far as I could see, a vast science-fiction machine, inventing a horrific other-world which would, at the end of the day, make you appreciate the not so bad space you inhabited. It endeavoured to placate with recipes and horoscopes. Have a cosy nightmare. It made you glad for your crippling mortgage, for your undamaged yet demanding children, for your crushing routine. Its world was populated by plastic personalities - waxy chat show hosts and bug-eyed personalities, vacuous manipulators, cancerous survivors and messianic soap-opera stars - in addition to the ram-raiders and ravaged royals, the fallen clergy and crazed ravers, street savages, gun-sellers and road-ragers. The latter included everybody who had a car now - all acting as they'd been told to do.

The relentless cosh of the column inch and news snippet - interspersed with those gardening hints and pennywise top tips - had created an atmosphere of bottled-up panic, in which all were mentally swinging out blindly at unseen terrors. This was no mean achievement as far as I could see. It made people relieved just to wake up alive with only their own tiny aches and feelings of apprehension, only the usual comparatively petty degradations. Their families, they would realise, filling their lungs with the choked optimism of dawn, were alive, their house was not razed to the ground. As if the jackboot had simply bounced off the door.

'So if we're the new lords of the manor, that makes your lot something like the church used to be,' I concluded, happy with this fanciful comparison, 'conjuring up the visions of hellfire and brimstone. You don't need the pulpits to make people afraid for their souls.'

I was doing all the talking by this time, and Jo Hinchcliffe must have been quite pissed off with me, but for reasons known only to herself allowed me, with hyped-up bravado, to kiss her then, like a teenager. This, I remember thinking, is something I bet Colin Chatterton, in his clown outfit, with his ear-stud and cigarillos, is in a position to do all the time. And Jimmy Raven, passing on all his worldly wisdom to those wide-eyed friends of his daughter, who followed him around like sheep.

Snogging, it was called in my day. It never occurred to me that her reasons were a mixture of self-sacrificing pity and blind ambition. I suppose that's why she slept with me too.

In doing so she taught me an important lesson: that after you reach a certain age, people respond to you largely for what you can give them, since there's really precious little they can give back to you.

The answer-phone was blinking happily as I stepped into the flat, but instead of the messages from Sally and Liz I hoped for, a succession of strangers spoke. The desk sergeant at the local police station asked me to get in contact concerning the car. Had Sally been in an accident? Nothing to worry about, he added, as if the recording could read my thoughts, merely a matter of procedure. There was a similar message from the Vehicle Licensing Office. A Mister Harris from an auditing firm called Sanderson Associates urged me to call him at my earliest convenience. He was slightly troubled by certain matters, he said, but felt sure I could straighten them out for him. Next was a bluff Yorkshireman whose name I didn't catch demanding to know 'what the bloody hell was going on', and then, inevitably, the bank.

I just couldn't deal with them, at that moment.

'You're popular,' Jo Hinchcliffe said, behind me.

I turned to discover she'd stripped down to her underwear, a black one-piece, resembling a 1950s swimming costume.

'So it seems.'

'Why don't we just forget about everything for a bit,' she suggested, 'since we're here anyway?'

Her arms curled around my neck and she kissed my ear. Her thighs were warm, and it struck me her hurry was merely a consequence of all that tension stoked up by the swathes of hatred flying about in The Wool Scourer; her contrasting languorousness the product of that Christmas syrup hanging like over-ripe vines from Wakefield's street lamps.

Then she bit my ear, hard enough to make me yelp.

'We could play rough if you like,' she said, 'get it all out of your system.'

I thought about the looks of admiration on the faces of those girls in the court-house, and it was obviously going to be nothing like the first time. But then, why would it be?

I folded my arms around her waist.

'Don't you have any furniture?' she asked, and although her eyes remained closed, her nose and lips did a disdainfully twitching reconnaissance of my quarters.

'I'm not interested in the trappings these days.'

She began unbuttoning my shirt and suddenly became convulsed by irritating laughter - all-pervading and instantly sobering.

'What?'

'What, he says.'

Her hand curled over her mouth and she stumbled backwards. 'Well, what?'

I hovered there, with my shirt unbuttoned down to my waist.

'You're wearing a vest.'

I glanced down with a hint of annoyance.

'A vest. Yes I am.'

'Well,' she began, and convulsed with laughter again, the absence of furniture preventing her from toppling into something.

'Well what?'

'Where do you buy them. Vests?'

'What can you mean?'

'Where can you get them, these days? Proper, old man's vests?'

I shrugged.

'Just the normal shops. Where people buy everything else, I suppose.'

'You don't even buy them for yourself then, somebody buys them for you?'

'I suppose they did.'

Jo Hinchcliffe slumped to the floor, verging on the hysterical. Then she looked up at me, with discernible pity in her eyes.

'They don't even make that kind of material, do they,' she said, 'anymore? God, you're a sad sack. I'm not sure this is going to work.'

Twenty

When I awoke the next morning, Jo Hinchcliffe had vanished without trace and, still half-asleep, I opened my door to Sergeant Dick Woolin and another police officer.

My first thought was that they were there in connection with the incident in The Wool Scourer on the previous afternoon, a notion probably prompted by a bruise to my cheek, caused more than likely by a stray elbow in the confusion, and until now anaesthetised. And then it struck me that it could be something to do with my appearance at the Gittings' household; that if Sally had got wind of the matter she would more than likely have sought to get the police involved, out of pure spite. This, I realised, was not an admirable record - two potential minor felonies in as many days, neither of them deliberate. Then I remembered the message about the car.

With a sense of relief I agreed with Woolin that I did own a red BMW with the registration he quoted, before it dawned on me that it was no longer true.

'Well,' I said, 'when you say 'own', what you probably mean is 'sponsor', do I tax it, foot its garage fees, fill it with petrol for some mystery man to continue his charged propulsions with my estranged wife therein? The answer is emphatically, yes.'

They exchanged wary nods, caps under arms, their identical uniforms compounded by corresponding raven-black New Romantic hairstyles - floppy fringed, cropped around the ears and twenty years out of date - although ludicrously, Woolin was a good six inches shorter and twenty years older than his partner. Who was also female.

'Can you tell us then,' the tall young woman clucked.

'Where you were,' Woolin continued.

'Yesterday?' they chorused.

'In service to the Crown,' I said, resisting the sudden urge to bow before them. 'I hope you haven't parked your Panda out front, I don't want all the curtains twitching.'

'Interesting,' the younger police officer confirmed, ignoring my last remark.

'And more than a coincidence, wouldn't you say Mr Turner?' and then he grinned. 'Know who this is, Forrester? A legend in law circles, and a firm friend of the force. A shark in the goldfish bowl of our resources.'

'Charming,' I said, flattered.

'This is Mister James Turner of the CPS.'

'Look, come in and tell me what you want.'

The place looked a tip, it struck me suddenly, despite its minimalism, as I surveyed it through the eyes of my visitors. But doubtless they'd seen worse than the burgeoning shoots of new bachelorhood represented by discarded beer cans, and items of clothing hanging limp on door handles.

Forrester looked puzzled and then extended her hand as she entered.

'Pleased to meet you Mister Turner, sir,' she said, in a tone that was a careful mix of deference and sarcasm, and then she started as a gust of harsh gibberish suddenly erupted from the walkie talkie attached to her lapel. She walked to the corner of the hall to fiddle with it.

'Take the weight off your feet for a while Sergeant,' I suggested, gesturing to the chair by the telephone. 'You look bushed. About to be out for the count, in fact.'

'I was just on my way home actually,' he said, sitting down and allowing his eyes to flutter shut for a couple of seconds.

'Hard shift?'

'Been on since ten last night,' he confirmed, refocusing.

'Overtime, then?'

I dipped into the kitchen with the wastepaper basket, removing foil trays and crumpled packets.

'I knew it was going to be one of those nights,' he shouted through to me, 'when somebody fell through a window at the Happy Chippy. There was an arson attack on the Pizza Hut and a virtual siege in the Wine Lodge.'

'Commerce at its most ferocious,' I replied, stepping back into the hall. 'And only a Wednesday.'

Forrester rejoined us, hovering and listening attentively.

Woolin turned to his colleague.

'We need more like him at the back of us Forrester, don't you forget that. One of the old school, he is.'

'We're awfully sorry to get you out of bed like this,' WPC Forrester said, anxiously seeking approval from the features of her Sergeant. 'We tried to contact you by phone first, but you don't seem to be here that often.'

I gave the magnanimous shrug of the busy man.

'I did get your message late last night, and intended to call this morning. Would you like tea or something?' I asked, which propelled Woolin back to his feet.

'No no, no need for anything like that.'

'You're sure?'

'Quite sure. We don't need to take up much of your time. It's just about your car. We had to move it, I'm afraid.'

'Slapped a sticker on it Monday,' Forrester said.

'It was up at the back of the council offices,' Woolin explained.

'On dotted yellows.'

'For three days.'

'And obviously you can't leave it there.'

'Certainly not overnight.'

They were lapsing into their double act again.

'I'm sure Mister Turner knows his Highway Code, Constable,' Woolin admonished, by way of re-establishing one-on-one conversation.

I shrugged.

'I don't know what to say,' I told him. 'If you had an inkling of the hassle she seems intent on causing. She probably didn't even need it in the first place, but took it anyway, along with the rest of the stuff. That's just typical of her, to dump it and put people out.'

'This is your wife?' Woolin asked searchingly.

'It is indeed. Certainly, my wife. But there's somebody else in the picture, too, I think you'll find.'

'She's left you?'

'Moved out last Sunday,' I confirmed. 'And cleaned me out while she was at it, lock, stock and barrel.'

'We'll need to talk to her then.'

'If you find out where she is, perhaps you could let me know. You could try her parents. They won't tell me anything, but you'd probably have more luck.'

Dutifully I scribbled down the Gittings' address, relishing the prospect of them pulling up on that street.

'To be honest, we thought it might have been stolen, hence the personal visit. It's in the compound now in any case, up at Wood Street, and since you're the legal owner you're quite entitled to come and collect it. Not that I want to interfere in personal matters. We had to satisfy ourselves there wasn't a bomb in it or anything, you understand. I have a sneaking suspicion your wife may have flooded the engine, in any case.'

We exchanged empathetic skyward glances. Forrester turned away, keeping her annoyance to herself.

'I suppose there's a fine to pay?'

'Unfortunately, yes.'

'Then she can deal with it herself,' I said, decisively. 'If independence is what she's seeking, then she'll have to learn to take the responsibility that goes with it.'

'As you wish. We'll call round at the address you've given us and see if we can contact her, then.'

'I'll give it till tomorrow and then if you've had no luck, I'll sort it out.'

They were edging towards the door now, and Woolin put on his hat.

'I'll tell you what,' he said, 'I only wish you could get a few more of the bastards banged up once we've apprehended them.'

I smiled at this remark, and so did he. We knew the score, our complicity told Forrester, us men, the lawmakers.

'And now I'm supposed to say there's always such a backlog and that for every prosecution that goes through there's another five pending.'

'Something like that. Of course, we've got the bloody festive season to look forward to next. That's always good for a bit more carnage. See you.'

I closed the door on them, and turning, recognised from the corner of my eye the shredded photographs on the floor of the toilet across the hall. I walked through and tried to remember the exact sequence of events which had resulted in me pulling them one by one from the collage the night before.

Jo Hinchcliffe had laughed at me, and I had no answer to that laughter. I was ridiculous.

In the toilet, the glass had fallen from the frame, for no reason whatsoever. Perhaps I had placed my hand against it to steady myself, or directed enough negative energy in its direction to cause vibrations.

Whatever, it simply fell at my feet, but didn't smash, despite the crack that was already there. I placed it carefully against the wall. My entire existence was some kind of joke, and the inexplicable breaking of the seal over that montage was confirmation of it. It seemed at that moment as if whatever I was striving for had never been worth the effort.

The picture of Sally and Jimmy making sandcastles on the beach at Robin Hood's Bay was the first to go. I ripped Kevin from his vainglorious corner, flicked the scrap down the bowl, and flushed. He surfed, then plummeted; resurfaced again. As the last trickles dribbled down the pan, he bobbed up breezily and settled on the surface. I was kneeling before the throne, wondering if I could be sick. Staring at my hands holding the torn photo. The jagged edge caused by Kevin's removal only served to fuel something. I cleaved the picture straight down the middle, and contemplated my son in one hand and my wife in the other, balancing the two. The scales of justice, the scales falling from my eyes. I dropped both pieces down into the toilet bowl and flushed again. When the falling water settled, they were all there, dancing happily together.

Jo Hinchcliffe knocked on the door, at that point. Curious. Perhaps even concerned. I just ignored her.

I stood up and pulled more pictures down from the frame. My parents, hers. The circumstantial evidence. These I shredded, five or six at a time, throwing them up in the air, so that they snowed around my ears.

After the police left that morning, I meticulously gathered them all up, as the phone began to ring again. I walked back into the hall, piecing the shrapnel of my rage into incoherent parts. My father's solemn features on the shoulders of Sally's party dress. The torso of her father juxtaposed against a line of pink eyes. A shotgun and a birthday cake.

I picked the phone up, placing these disembodied images down on the table next to it.

'What the hell do you think you're playing at?'

My wife was the last person I expected, and the venom in her tone was the hair of a dog which had bitten me.

'Sally?'

My voice came out meek and guilty, serving to reinforce her indignation.

'What on earth were you doing round at my parents?'

'I wanted to see my son,' I replied quickly. I had the clump of shredded photos cupped in my hand. The next three I put down were parts of James Junior. His sprouting legs, knees patched in the image of *Thomas the Tank Engine*, his tiny hands cupped around a feeding bottle, his sleeping face.

'What's got into you?' she demanded.

'Where are you?' I asked her.

'Never mind that, how did my father get that mark on his face? Did you hit him?'

'No of course not. Don't be stupid.'

She let the silence down the line between us reinforce the accusation then, a suspended moment in which I waited for the gavel to fall.

'Where are you phoning from?' I asked again, finally, when it became overbearing.

'Tell me the truth.'

Her voice was distant, suddenly drained of its anger.

'I didn't hit him, he sort of stumbled,' I said.

'That's what he said, though I don't see why he'd want to protect you.'

'Because it's the truth.'

She said nothing in reply to this. I pressed my head against the wall as the seconds of passing silence began to rush and boom in my ears again. 'Are you still there?'

'You were pissed, weren't you?'

'I'd had a couple, that's all. I just wanted to see Jimmy.'

'You haven't taken any notice of him for months. God, James.'

'Well where were *you*?'

'I told them I'd be back for him yesterday. Just a few days was all I needed. I don't know why they had to see you. I suppose they were trying to help. Look, you've got to get a grip.'

Sally would have been staring up at me from the next scrap I put down on the table, if her eyes hadn't been closed. Her easy laughter ran through my head as I remembered the time we spent decorating that bedroom for the arrival of our son. It should have been a simple matter, keeping that laughter going, keeping it close. I plunged the remaining Kodachrome scraps into my pocket.

'I didn't hit your dad,' I said. 'I wouldn't do that.'

She sighed, which I took to be an indication she wanted to believe me.

'Is everything else okay?' she asked.

'Oh, fine and dandy. Everything's just great. Why wouldn't it be? I've just had the police round, for one thing.'

'Why?'

'About the bloody car. You left it on Wood Street didn't you?'

'I didn't take the car.'

'Come on, Sally, don't piss me about. Who's there with you now?'

'I'm not with anyone.'

'Where is he then?'

'Who, Jimmy?'

'No, not Jimmy, whoever it is. Your mystery man.'

Having said this, I instantly realised the trap I'd fallen into. It was my son I was supposed to be concerned about.

'Dad said this too, that you'd said all this nonsense. Were you drunk again anyway, is that it? And forgot where you'd left it?'

'What?'

'The car, of course.'

'Who's with you?'

She sighed and there was a momentary wave of crackling interference, as if she was moving the receiver, or holding her hand over it or something. A gust of wind buffeted against the front door at my side, and the mat under it shivered.

'I'll put the phone down if you carry on,' she said. 'That's a promise. Look, I stayed with a friend for a few days, that's all. They looked after Jimmy for me.'

'Really?'

'I stayed with Liz Armstrong.'

'Oh, great.'

This provided an opportunity for me to let a stretch of silence work in my favour. I closed my eyes, willing a little of the anger and guilt back in her direction. An image loomed up, of the two women laughing away helplessly in the lounge, the previous Sunday. Sally pushing her finger to her nose on the sofa, Liz down on the carpet in the litter of toys.

'I just needed to be away from everything,' Sally said. 'Away from the house.' Away from *you*, was what she was implying. 'I don't know that many people these days, do I?'

'I suppose that's my fault as well,' I replied, suddenly more annoyed than the situation warranted. But when it came down to it, what did I ask of her? What, for that matter, did I ask of anyone? Why was it that disapproval of my behaviour should be voiced so easily, that my character flaws should be the focus of such attention? When did I lay the blame? When did I allow myself to criticise and judge in such an easy fashion?

'And you're thinking of coming back now, is that it?' I said, with an inexplicable sense of triumph, which turned out to be completely misplaced.

'No,' she said, decisively, as if it was the question she'd been waiting to hear. As if I'd actually phoned *her*, to ask it. 'I'm not coming back. That's not a good idea, is it? Perhaps it will be, later, but I don't know now.'

'Not now that Liz has pumped you full of her poison. And dear old Mum and Dad.'

'I didn't phone to talk about us.'

'Well what did you phone for?'

'To find out what happened. And, well, something else. About Liz, I suppose, though I don't see why I should care less.'

'Oh, great.'

'No, listen, did you look through those papers she gave you to sign?'

'Of course I did, it's all being sorted out. God, Sal, do you think I don't understand these things?'

'It's just...while I was there she opened up to me a bit.'

'I don't believe we're having a conversation about Liz bloody Armstrong when there's all this between us.'

'Well I don't know, something didn't seem right to me. Her house has been sold you know. It was the way she deliberately avoided the subject when I asked her. If you were moving, you'd want to talk about it wouldn't you? Anyway, yesterday I bumped into Franklin.'

'That old fool.'

'He thinks she's been given too much of a free rein with things. That she's been making bad decisions.'

'He's just living in the past.'

'Then, remember she said Franklin was on holiday? Well that wasn't true, either.'

'I know that. She'd got it wrong. It's not hard to misunderstand him.'

'Franklin said he thought she was deliberately avoiding people.'

'Oh, who cares? Forget about the business, I've already informed her I want out. And I mean completely out. That's probably why she's in a tiz.'

'Can you just do that, though?'

'Of course I can.'

'Well, if you're sure.'

'I am. Look, we should meet.'

There was another long pause, as if she was considering this.

'Not now James.'

'Well, when then?'

'I don't know yet. Just give it time.'

'When I find out who it is...'

'I'm putting the phone down now. Take care.'

She did. I stared at the receiver, trying to figure out what was going on, listening to the unbroken signal. My eyes alighted on a pile of travel brochures heaped at the side of the door. I couldn't remember collecting them, but the idea of jetting off somewhere for Christmas had been on my mind for a few days at least, to get away from everything. I sat down and scanned them: Rio, Jamaica, Singapore, Thailand - anywhere without the tinsel and trappings. With a full three weeks before the resumption of my court duties there was nothing to stop me and certainly nothing to keep me at home. I decided to act immediately and go and buy a ticket.

Twenty-one

It was one of those winter days when it never quite becomes daylight, and a vicious wind was punching everything in its path, beating a line of fast-food cartons and fliers down to the canal below the station. The sun was an indistinct shape behind a sky like an x-ray of internal organs. I had decided to opt for somewhere I could perhaps enjoy a Christmas Day barbecue on the beach, or at least feel the sun, without having first to endure a flight of more than four hours. This, I decided, would limit me to the outer fringes of Europe, to Turkey or North Africa, but I was willing to put up with the Islamic idiosyncrasies of those countries, provided I could find a suitably civilised and fenced-off hotel complex.

I do not travel well. Like Samuel Johnson I would prefer to lie on a chaise-longue as the world's riches are paraded in front of me. My complexion is not particularly suited to the sun, and on one occasion in Greece I got too much of it. My shoulders bubbled up with painful sacks of jelly and I was obliged to spend the remaining days of our stay mummified by towels and huddled under the shadow of a rock. I hate airports, of course, with their myriad rituals, bewildering labyrinths and confused, overburdened and inappropriately dressed crowds. The sinisterly painted young women in the booths and the uniformed officials taking away your identity and belongings for private inspection. And all of this a preface to being voluntarily strapped in to a metal shell which will subsequently be hurtled into the stratosphere. There is the possibility of losing everything in airports - your destination, your liberty, your marbles.

All of these misgivings I was determined to overcome. As I walked up Westgate however, I was suddenly stopped in my tracks as I passed the front window of a rather pretentious establishment called 'Curiosities'. I stared inside, astonished.

There is a distinction between objects which will appreciate in value in time due to their craftsmanship and quality, and those which have simply reached a ripe age by chance. 'Curiosities' specialised in the latter. Had it professed to sell vintage wines, its window would have been racked with dusty bottles of Double Diamond and Jubilee Stout. As a men's outfitters, wide lapels and polyester would have been the order of the day. No serious collector would have gone near it.

By coincidence, the owner of this shop, Ansell Simmonds, had been employed by me a few months before, in his other capacity as a tree surgeon, to fell a row of conifers which were blocking out the light to the conservatory I intended to have erected. Simmonds informed me he could have provided the conservatory for a fraction of what its professional erection would cost, but for some reason I declined this offer.

I was staring at two chandeliers dangling precariously above the usual bric-a-brac. They were decorated with a vile assortment of scarves and ties, but they were undoubtedly the same pair which had graced my house until less than a fortnight ago, when Sally saw fit to strip the place. She had no right to them whatsoever, and was surely aware of that. Knowing her somewhat reticent nature, it wouldn't have surprised me at all to learn she had been prompted by whoever she was with to take more than was hers.

The chandeliers had been bequeathed to me by my father, specified in his will, and had dangled above me over many laborious meal-times as a child. At Christmas they became magical. They gave off a peculiar multi-hued glow reminiscent of the stained glass windows of churches, which was perhaps to do with the quality of light and the presence of candles at that time of year.

I stood outside the shop, still staring, falling back into the past.

My father decided to take me into York on Christmas Eve. I remembered us pulling up ostentatiously outside a toy and book shop, a fuzz of pipe smoke jetting into the steely white cobbled street as we climbed down from the Land Rover. Once inside the shop, however, we were both of us lost, in terms of actually buying something.

'It's Christmas, son,' my father said to me, 'I have to get you something. So what do you want?'

I tinkered with trains and dabbled with *Dinky* cars, tried on boxing gloves and football boots, but the truth was, I didn't want anything the shop had. Everything I touched had my father reaching magnanimously for his cheque book. He was as lost as I was, there. We both wanted more from each other. He was not seeking to buy me off, and I was not willing to settle for trinkets.

Finally, he became irritated.

'It's Christmas,' he repeated, the calm in his voice strained. 'You've got to have things.'

I wanted his love, nothing else. I can say it now, now that it is not swaggering towards me, threatening to knock me over again. Nothing else would do. By not wanting anything, by rising above it, I was seeking to be like him, and to show him I was that chip off the old block. Instead I quickly annoyed him. I was eventually whisked off in a cloud of pipe smoke, presentless. There was a parking ticket on the Land Rover when we got back to it, and it was implicit that my hesitancy was the cause of it. My father ripped it into tiny pieces and flung it into the air so that it snowed around my ears. There were subdued tears on my part and recriminations on his, as we headed frostily back home.

Slowly recovering myself, I now spotted a china tea service in the window of 'Curiosities', underneath the two chandeliers. This had also belonged to the Turners for generations and was certainly out of place amongst the junk which constituted the rest of the stock. Dismayed, I entered the shop to be casually greeted by Ansell Simmonds, who was perched on a hard-backed chair, smoking a cigarette. At that very moment I noticed a line of ash about to fall from his tube of poison onto the elaborate Persian rug below him, and dived to prevent such an abomination. Startled, Simmonds shot to his feet.

'This isn't something you stand on, for God's sake, you barbarian,' I shouted, grappling at his ankles and rolling the rug away from him.

His initial bewilderment gave way to a shrewd and calculating look, squinting through his smoke.

'Mister Turner,' he said, 'funnily enough I thought of you when that piece came in. Fifty notes, and it's yours.'

'It is mine, in any case. Where did you get it? She didn't bring it in herself surely?'

I propped the rolled up rug against a dud stereo rack system.

'Who's that then?'

'My wife, of course.'

'Mrs Turner?' He scratched his chin thoughtfully. 'You know, I don't think she's ever been down here, now you mention it. Which is a shame, a real shame. I reckon there'd be plenty that would catch her eye.'

My suspicion deepened.

'How do you know my wife?'

He shrugged expansively.

'I've been to your house of course, haven't I. Remember? She had to come out and restrain that daft dog of yours, once I got the saw going. Lovely creature, though. The dog, I mean, not that your wife's not...'

'This is my property,' I told him. 'The rug, those chandeliers in the window, and that tea service. I want to know what they're doing in this pit.'

'Calm down Mister Turner,' Simmonds said then. 'You'll do yourself an injury, getting all worked up like this. It certainly wasn't Mrs Turner who sold me them. And I've got receipts, in case you were wondering. All above board.'

He was a shabby individual up close, with slightly popping eyes and a nicotine-stained moustache. It was his manner however, ingratiating and wheedling, I found infuriating. Then another idea struck me.

'Was it a man who sold you them?'

'Well...'

'Come on, I haven't got all day to stand around here.'

'Yes,' Simmonds agreed, 'it was. A man.'

'What did he look like?'

'I'm not sure I can reveal my sources.'

'Just tell me.'

'Not your type at all. Just an average punter, really.'

'Young?'

'Uh-huh. Early twenties I suppose.'

So Sally was running around with someone barely out of his teens, a toy-boy, as those grizzled perpetrators of Jo Hinchcliffe's profession would have it. I felt a sudden twinge of pity for Sally. It was all rather pathetic, wasn't it? Undoubtedly, in part, her deception had been motivated by feelings of fear and trepidation, of the niggling apprehension of the on-set of menopause. Sad, if not tragic, when I thought about it. But to have run off with some boy, and not only that, to have encouraged him to sell my belongings to a jumped up rag and bone man for small change, was way beyond the pale.

The train of my suspicions as to the identity of her Mr X, which had revolved around a narrow track up to that point, was promptly derailed. None of the faces would fit all of a sudden, and I was at a loss for volunteers to populate my new identity parade - an indistinct line of bum-fluff and pimples. Who did she know in their early twenties? The window cleaner perhaps, the son of one of our acquaintances? To have been betrayed, abandoned and cleaned out was one thing, but this latest revelation held the potential for something much more embarrassing, both personally and socially. And then I remembered the gym. It had to be someone she'd met there.

As calmly as I could, I explained again to Ansell Simmonds that whoever had sold him the things was not authorised to do so. They were not his to sell. I assured him I would resolve the matter as soon as possible and made him promise not to attempt to sell them in the mean time, agreeing that he would be reimbursed in full and threatening to bring the full weight of the law down on his stooped shoulders should he do otherwise.

'What about clarinets?'

'Clarinets?'

'Did he sell you a pair of clarinets?'

'I don't do musical instruments. No demand round here.'

Breathlessly I left 'Curiosities' and was blown half way back to the railway station before I remembered the actual reason for my journey into town.

I walked into the first travel agency I could find, and was eventually cheered by the rapt attention of the pretty clerk, and by the blue-skied, sun-kissed panoramas in the brochures we leafed through together. The beggars and the restaurant hawkers had been carefully air-brushed from every one.

'Your Sunsets sales executive is Dawn', the badge on her bottle green blazer informed me, and her immaculately manicured scarlet nails clicked on the computer keyboard as she began tracking down vacancies. The way she bit her bottom lip in concentration made me delay over my selection, moved by the sincerity of her limited knowledge. One resort was good for bargains in leather goods apparently, but they expected you to barter; another was famous for its volcanic springs and a lethal cherry brandy; the night life was muted here, the hospitality legendary there.

I pictured Dawn on the bus to work, memorising snippets from brochures for the entertainment of her clients. This I found a moving image.

Finally, I selected a two week stay in southern Turkey at a private-seeming establishment fringed by lush greenery and overlooking the sea. I pictured myself on its tiny balcony, a glass in hand, contentedly watching the sky darken, the calls of the muezzin issuing from the golden dome concealed somewhere behind a tangle of flat white roofs on the horizon.

Dawn happily punched through all the booking details, which took her a considerable amount of time. It was with some relief I could finally hand her my Master Card to enable the deal to be concluded.

I really needed the break, I realised then. Holidays always provided me with the stamina to bounce back fighting. In fact, after just a couple of days, my head was usually so full of plans to be instigated I became unhappy to be away from the cut and thrust of home. I would rediscover my perspective; of that I was certain.

Perhaps I'd make notes for myself and plan out some kind of positive future; a definite direction.

Dawn retreated into a back room to phone through my details, so that I could just see her pleasantly tanned legs - legs that longed to be on foreign beaches - swinging from the chair through the door as she trilled down the phone.

When she returned, there was a sudden edginess to her immaculately touched-up features.

'I'm afraid they won't authorise me to process payment,' she said. Did I notice a little flicker of hardness in her eyes then, something ever so slightly prim and accusing in her tone?

'I'm sorry,' I replied, 'who won't authorise what?'

'The payment, Mr Turner. Your credit company.'

I chuckled paternally at her anxiety.

'But it's a mistake, surely,' I said, 'Why on earth wouldn't they do so?'

'Have you got sufficient credit in?' Dawn asked gently. I found her sincerity touching again, and was happy to dismiss the impression that she was somehow patronising me. Giving her my best captain-of-industry smile of reassurance, I opened my wallet again.

'Well, well,' I said, 'somebody's being very inefficient, aren't they? Too much paperwork I suspect, computers left to reach their own decisions. It's always the way in these big organisations. Heads have certainly rolled for less. Now I suppose I shall have to write them a nasty letter to get to the bottom of it...now let's see what we've got here, shall we.'

She smiled at the familiar hologram which glistened in the corner of my American Express card.

Two minutes later she was back again.

'The account has been cancelled. They'd like to speak to you personally.'

I walked through into the back room and took the phone. The clerk droned on about the necessity of making regular payments and clearing an unauthorised overdraft, and I attempted to make the appropriate noises without unnecessarily disturbing Dawn. A couple entered the shop then, and as Dawn turned on her heels I cut off the caller and barked commandingly that the service I had recently been receiving was unforgivable.

'Well I want it sorting, and I want it sorting now,' I shouted.

I hovered there then, behind the door, as Dawn went through details with her new customers. When they finally left, I stepped out.

'I'm afraid there's a problem, Dawn,' I said, 'but believe me, I've given them what for. I'll have to come back tomorrow now.'

Twenty-two

It was Friday, and the historian's initial call was early.

'James, have you seen the paper yet?' he said, sounding irritatingly lively.

'I'm not even out of bed.'

'Rouse yourself then, at once, I'll bring it around.'

'Why? I'm not interested.'

'You're on the front page. They're making accusations.'

'What? What about?'

'Somebody called Chatterton.'

'Colin Chatterton?'

'You'll need to see it, and think what to do. I'll be half an hour, at the most.'

Christ, Chatterton, it seemed, was out to crucify me. I dressed and pottered into the kitchen, turned the kettle on and put a carton of milk to my lips only to be immediately alerted to its rancid smell. I scooped down a handful of dry cereal from a box lying on its side, tipped the remains of a jar of Nescafé into a bowl and poured boiling water on to it, then paced the cushion floor, thinking.

My night had been a fitful one, burdened as I was with rather too much to think about. First, having posted the bulk of my financial papers to Liz Armstrong, rather hastily I realised, I had no way of finding an explanation for either Sally's misgivings about her, or that humiliating rigmarole in the travel agency. It was akin to those occasional dreams of suddenly being naked in a supermarket. I had never been refused credit before, anywhere, nor had I been placed in a situation in which a shop-girl, however attractive, had found herself suddenly in a position to judge me. She had looked down her nose from an elevated position while I fumbled through my wallet, my gushing attempts to gain control of the situation ringing completely hollow.

I had to meet Liz soon, that much was apparent. Sort things out. Get it all in black and white, finalised.

I had certainly never needed to examine my personal bills too closely when they arrived, like some sordid accounts clerk. The way it worked was that Sally would go through them and I would sign whatever cheques were necessary. Women, I had always thought, understood such things. They liked to study lists, to itemise and organise. Regardless of whether it was Liz Armstrong or Sally, I was happy to leave all the small print to them.

I heard the postman depositing another load onto the hall carpet with a significant flourish at that moment.

There was the matter of my family heirlooms suddenly lurching towards me in the front of that squalid little shop, and what Ansell Simmonds had said. A young man had brought them in. I couldn't help picturing some lithe Adonis with even features and surf-bleached hair, all frayed jeans and gel. But the image, I knew, was preposterous.

What about Alan, then, Sally's brother? He hated me, I knew. But it struck me that Sally and her immediate family were hardly in need of ready cash. What if their assertions were true? What if they were nothing to do with it?

The thing was, I didn't know where to turn next, what plan of action to formulate. It made me feel inadequate. My father would never have allowed himself to be put in such a position of indecisiveness.

I walked into the hall with the bowl to my lips and immediately a light blue Air Mail letter vied for my attention in the mess of official-looking envelopes under the letterbox. I set the bowl down on the carpet and picked it up. A row of Australian flags danced across the stamps at one edge. There was something evocative about the arrangement of stars in seas of blue. Unfamiliar with the wafery paper and complicated sealing arrangement, however, I succeeded in my eagerness to obliterate half of the ink as I tore the letter apart.

...a bit out of the blue was the first legible phrase.

I work in the bar of a hotel in Canberra now. It's okay. Things are more laid-back over here. I'll never come back, anyway. When I think of England I just think of how small everything seemed, somehow, and the rain and cold. I think it does something to the people, that climate. Stunts you, makes you bitter and resigned to things. There's a feeling that nothing will change for the better, regardless of how hard you try. I won't sicken you with any stories about barbecues on the beach because I know only too well what it's like there in December.

I only discovered your address by accident. It's been a long time, and I am 9,000 miles away after all. Your father always said you'd be a solicitor. I've thought about writing many times in the past. I went as far as phoning the Crown Prosecution Service in London and they confirmed you were on their register. They wouldn't give out your address, so I left it. For ages. And God knows I've got enough to feel guilty about anyway. I haven't been in touch with them in all this time, you see. Not since your father gave me the money to leave.

But about a year ago I served late drinks to some solicitor from Yorkshire for a week or so. He spotted my accent straight away. Well, you don't lose it, do you? He was just on holiday with his wife, but your name leapt into my head and he said he thought he'd once defended a case against you. So there you are. They were pissed, this solicitor guy and his wife, one night. I pressed it, and he throws some little black book out onto the bar. And sure enough, there's your name and address. I didn't even write it down, just put it in my head.

James, if it is you, how are you? Perhaps you never think about me. You were constantly held up as an example, though. We lived on your land of course. When I think of that hateful cottage now I can hardly believe we put up with being so cramped. And I'd look out of the window at your huge farmhouse and they'd tell me about how well you were doing at your private school, that you were captain of the rugby team and would go far. I came to quite despise your name. I know that's not your fault.

Anyway, as I say, it was your father who gave me the money to come out here. You are doubtless asking yourself why he did that, since he was hardly generosity itself. He wouldn't provide me with any explanation, nor would my mother. What do you remember about it all, the way our parents were, back then? Your father storming about the place, everybody scared of him. There are things I think I remember but won't allow to become focused. As I got older and probably more capable of understanding, the visits stopped. And then, all those years later, he turned up without an explanation and wrote me a cheque. Just like that. I'd been arguing with Dad all the time and I was desperate to get away from that cottage and Yorkshire. I had this crap job sorting mushrooms and my prospects were bleak. I can only think now that my mother must have talked to him, but at the time I just saw the opportunity and grabbed it.

To my shame, I haven't been in touch with them for the last decade. They can hardly read, for one thing, and I was angry with them for a long time. I know this might seem like a cheek, and probably quite cowardly, but if you can, James, could you do something...

The legible part of the letter stopped there and a sprightly knock on the door, inches away from my face, announced the historian's arrival. I scooped up the bowl, stood up and opened the door.

'James,' he said gravely. The mark on his cheek, I noticed, was rapidly subsiding. He handed me the scrolled paper.

I sat down at the kitchen table and he sat opposite, examining my face for a reaction as I first surveyed the headline.

INJUSTICE? THAT WILL DO NICELY, SAYS TOP POLICE LAWYER

Of the 350,000 or so people who inhabit a city and its surrounding area such as Wakefield, perhaps a seventh take the local paper.

Of that seventh, that fifty thousand, perhaps one in a hundred bother to read it from cover to cover. Most make do with skimming the sports pages, scanning the jobs section or poring over the classified ads in search of a second-hand car or a reputable plumber. The older end turn straight to the obituaries in anticipation of the morbid thrill of identifying an old acquaintance who should not be forgot, whilst in a similar vein those further from death's door seek out a familiar face in the parade of weekend weddings or the truncated reports of drink-drive offenders. And those remaining five hundred avid readers, they largely constitute the non-decision makers; the people with too much time on their hands: lonely pensioners and the unemployed, in hostels and libraries, bed-sits and greasy spoons. Sally's father, of course, was compelled to commit every story, however trivial, to the fathomless archive in his head.

Who indeed can recall the headline story from their local paper last week, let alone a year or even a month ago?

But sometimes a local story, however apparently innocuous and parochial, however lacking in substance, can transcend the genre and travel supersonic and first class. Its routes will be multifarious and far-reaching: down the fax machines of bored executives, between the departments of relevant institutions, e-mailed or telexed through the communications networks of international news agencies who sense its potential; incensed memos and reports, fodder for bemused diary pieces and cynical sound bites, after dinner conversation and corridor chat.

The story in question was not really a story at all, simply a cobbling together of common concerns and coincidences united by a solitary thread. And that thread happened to be my wayward train of thought as I accompanied Jo Hinchcliffe from the court steps to the pub called The Wool Scourer on that eventful Wednesday afternoon following the Raven and Pickles trial, exactly a week before Christmas Day.

It would not, usually, have taken up such space in a local family newspaper, had it not arrived at a timely stage in the organ's development, running parallel to a revamped, harder-hitting, concerted attempt to boost circulation under new editorial control. And Jo Hinchcliffe's powers of persuasion surely played their part. That night, she slept with me. Thursday, as I spoke first to the police officers and then Sally, she was writing it all up. Doubtless having conversed with her editor.

By the time I was staring into the window of 'Curiosities', or at least as I left the travel agents, it must have been on the page. Neat work.

It wasn't that the opinions attributed to me were particularly controversial. Far from it. They were, give or take the odd learned allusion or fanciful quote, the opinions of that bulk which constitutes the middle ground: policemen certainly, magistrates, bankers and businessmen, but road-sweepers and hot-dog vendors too. Blue and white collar together, indignant fathers cursing at the evening news over their dinner trays, chewing the fat with neighbours across hedges, in their local pubs, getting furious as the liquor loosened their tongues, bewildered and prone to free-floating anxiety attacks in their cars and on trains, in changing rooms, potting sheds, clubs and institutions nationwide.

They were not really even opinions at all, but simply shocked reactions; the twitchings of traumatised nerve ends in response to the seeming intransigence of a hard world. Like most people I have developed a hard outer shell simply to protect a soft centre. More than anything, I crave empty courtrooms, a utopia where all are responsible for their own actions - principled, fair, and perhaps above all, solvent.

As I read, I felt a sort of numb recognition. The contents of the piece were bringing with them the events of the last few days with a clarity I had sought to blank out with alcohol and pain.

The first thing was the photograph of myself. This had been stolen, presumably by Jo Hinchcliffe, from what remained of the montage in my toilet. One of the few I hadn't shredded. It was the one where I had my eyes half closed and was grappling with something out of the picture. Out of context the image made me look remedially psychopathic; a man beyond help. Next was a picture of Colin Chatterton, in sunglasses and a loud open-necked shirt, looking like a Miami drug dealer. There was a cropped picture of Sally too, with her eyes shut. Underneath this, the one word caption was 'Divorcing'.

In a block column to the left of these pictures was the following question:

MUST THE INNOCENT SUFFER
AT THE HANDS OF THE CORRUPT?

The word 'innocent' made me smile, with its biblical connotations. The historian shook his head and fumbled up at me, placing a hand on my shoulder and asking where I kept the tea-bags these days. I read on:

An official complaint to the Law Society is to be made by a local Legal Aid defence solicitor against his counterpart in the Crime Prosecution Service.

Mr Colin Chatterton is to ask for a prompt investigation at the highest level into the events following a magistrates' court hearing which took place on Wednesday this week.

James Hartley Turner is very much a member of the establishment, and paid handsomely for his wisdom. Often his powers of persuasion are responsible for the sentences delivered by well-meaning magistrates (who give up their own valuable time to sit on the Bench) in cases connected to events in this city. And yet his opinions on modern British society, and in particular on the role of the authorities, would shame a meeting of wild extremists. A vociferous advocate of family values whose own marriage has, according to his estranged wife, been irreparably damaged by his inconsiderate behaviour, Turner must be viewed as nothing less than a potential danger to the public.

Whether or not he should remain in his present position is a question his superiors must surely consider very carefully. Mr Chatterton's allegations will be landing on the desk of the Director of Public Prosecutions this morning.

'I have known Mr Turner for many years,' said Mr Chatterton, 'but I have to say his attitude has become less and less acceptable in a modern courtroom. Of all our institutions, this is the one with the most exacting guidelines set in place, so there is little excuse for brazenly flaunting the rules in an attempt to have your own way, regardless of the outcome. He seems no longer interested in justice, but merely in seeking a result.'

One victim of Turner's abrasive style is 21-year-old local student, Ronald Pickles, who on Wednesday was ordered to carry out Community Service work for a minor drugs offence. Like many youngsters these days, Mr Pickles was drawn into the shady netherworld of drugs by peer pressure, realising his mistake too late to avoid trouble. Mr Pickles had, at the same court hearing, been cleared of having any involvement in a shocking burglary which took place over a year ago. Having endured the disgrace of being wrongfully accused for the past twelve months, he was more than anxious to get the case over and done with. In the event, the magistrates were not swayed by the blistering invective of Mr Turner and were more than happy to erase the name of Mr Pickles, and his friend Mr James Raven, from the list of suspects for that robbery in open court. Mr Turner was less than pleased with their decision.

What he did next was beyond belief. In a Wakefield public house, the Crown Prosecution Service lawyer was instrumental in starting a brawl.

'We were just playing a game of pool, me and Jimmy,' a shocked Ronald Pickles explained yesterday. 'And suddenly Mr Turner was there shouting at us. He was swearing about Mr Chatterton and became quite aggressive. He was asked to leave, but refused. He continued to shout and swear at us, however, until members of staff forcibly removed him from the premises. It was all very upsetting after what Jimmy and I had been through.'

One woman who knows better than anyone about Turner's unpredictable mood swings and erratic behaviour is his wife, Sally. Mrs Turner is believed to be lodging divorce proceedings against her husband.

'I don't want to talk about James, if you don't mind,' she said yesterday. 'The man is simply unhinged.'

Nor are the police particularly happy about his methods. One constable, who wished to remain anonymous, was contemptuous of the procedural practices employed by Turner, and of his attitude, which she described as 'Neanderthal and very much old boys' club'. He would insist on meeting before particular cases, it was alleged...

This was simple character assassination, nothing more. I wanted to laugh out loud at the way I was being used by Jo Hinchcliffe, and by Chatterton, and by Pickles and Raven.

The historian placed a mug of tea down at my side and put his hand on my shoulder.

'This is what it's like in history,' he chirped, in that tone of peculiar optimism he adopted whenever he was being gloomy. 'The actual events which constitute the factual meat are malleable. They can be stretched to fit theories, and squeezed into holes. Who knows how it will all appear, a hundred years from now.'

He sat opposite me and I felt suddenly sorry for him. Or perhaps for myself. He looked down into his own mug, stirring the tea with a spoon absently. His legs began to tremble, not through nerves, but self-absorption, through becoming lost in his thoughts again. Here was a man the very opposite of my father. Not a success, nor perhaps satisfied. But he'd managed to keep a happy family and make a living out of simple curiosity and a willingness to know more.

I put the paper down, reluctant to read on, going over and unplugging the phone from the wall. My career was in jeopardy, I realised, imagining certain individuals who considered themselves my peers choking on their toast within the hour. The knives would be out.

I saw Jo Hinchcliffe's article pinned to notice-boards: in the court house, the police station, the office of my practice, my gormless face in that inappropriate photograph appended with shaky felt-tip glasses, a Groucho Marx moustache, a pair of devil's horns...

'Do you think I'm unhinged?' I asked the historian.

He looked at me directly for the first time.

'You've made my daughter very unhappy, I know that.'

'So she told you about it.'

'And you won't be able to make her happy again, whatever happens now.'

'I knew you were all in it together from the start. One big happy family. It's all right for some.'

He closed his eyes, shaking his head with uncharacteristic annoyance.

'You have a family too.'

'Not now.'

'Nobody's in anything together, James. She came back yesterday. She'll be staying with us for a while now. Until after Christmas, or until she decides what she wants to do.'

'Whirlwind romance over, is it? Toy-boy moved on to pastures new?'

The historian got to his feet.

'There hasn't been anything going on. She's upset and confused, that's all.'

'What about Jimmy?' I asked, as the smiling face of my son came suddenly into my mind.

'The proverbial Tasman Devil. Don't worry about him.'

Somebody knocked on the door.

'You get it. Tell them I'm not here.'

'You'll have to face up to it sooner or later.'

'But not yet, put them off for me.'

'I don't like lying for anyone.'

'Please.'

'Sally said that on the night you argued, she finally came to the decision she was leaving you for good. She said you were drunk and that you'd said a lot of hurtful things. She also said...and I know this can't be true...that you killed the dog, or that you paid somebody to do it. The farmhand, what's his name? He shot him. Is that right?'

'It was a mistake, an over-reaction. Nothing to do with me. You don't honestly think it was, do you?'

His kindly eyes burned into mine.

'I really don't know.'

Reluctantly he rose and went to answer the door.

'Hello again.'

The familiar voice of Sergeant Dick Woolin.

'You've told him about the car then.' Woolin said as the two entered.

'Not yet,' the historian said. 'It was one of the things we were getting around to. James has had a bit of bad news.' He indicated the newspaper on the table. Uninvited, Woolin picked it up.

First he laughed, then tutted, and then cursed, as he read.

'Not exactly the kindest likeness,' he said, thrusting that cursed photo at me again. 'They're a set of bastards, all of them. Especially Chatterton. Jumped-up little do-gooder. Don't take it to heart though. Did you really start a punch-up in the Scourer? You certainly pick your spots. What were you doing in there anyway?'

'Having a drink'

'I wouldn't have thought it was your kind of place?'

'It's a free country.'

'You were with the reporter, right, Jo Hinchcliffe, who wrote this?'

He sat down opposite me, in the seat Sally's father had vacated. He looked even more tired than he had the previous day, as if he hadn't slept since. An unwashed smell came from him.

'Like I say, it's a free country.'

'They'll have your balls, you know that? But anyway, I came about the car. Your wife, it seems, never moved it from outside this door. So tell me, what's been going on?'

Twenty-three

'Mrs Turner maintains that she never took your car,' Woolin said as we climbed into his. 'So how did it come to be where it was, that's all I want to know. Did it get there on its own? What I'm asking is, I suppose, have you been straight with us about everything, Mr Turner?'

'Of course I have.' I wasn't in the mood for his questions and there was little of the deference in his voice that had existed previously.

'Well, things don't add up somehow,' he said. 'Could it have been stolen? Or were you perhaps a little agitated when you left it there? A man in your position has to be cautious. That must be very apparent now. Had too much to drink?'

'She took it. Whatever she says. She's lying.'

'Her father says she couldn't drive it, didn't like to. It was too big for her. She was scared of it.'

'So how did she move everything out?'

'She says she never took anything.'

'He took it then, the boyfriend. Drove it for her.'

Woolin shook his head.

'There isn't a boyfriend, if her father's to be believed, and he's hardly the lying sort.'

'Oh, I see. The entire family is beyond reproach, is that it? I'd like to think I was held in the same esteem, given so much benefit of the doubt. What about her brother, Alan, for instance?'

He shook his head.

'Tell me about that incident in the Scourer. What was that all about?'

'I was just angry, I suppose. About the case. You know how it is. They were as guilty as sin, you know as well as I do.'

'And that's the first time you met the two of them, is it, in court?'

'I know Raven of course, we all do, don't we? The good old Blue Crooner?'

He looked at me dubiously. There were to be no fond anecdotes.

'But you never met Ronald Pickles before?'

'No. Why would I?'

'It's just that last Saturday he happened to make allegations against you. Said, actually, that you assaulted him. Walked right into the station and filed a complaint, bold as brass. The desk clerk laughed it off of course, but a couple of the lads promised to follow it up. Just to get rid of him, I suppose. He said he'd been to see Chatterton too, but we never heard from him. Of course, with so much paperwork it never came to light that you were in charge of the case against him on Wednesday. Chatterton would have known, of course, and used it to weaken the case if he'd had to.'

'So?'

'You just said you never met him.'

'He tried to mug me.'

'So you did know him. When was that?'

'The night before he filed the complaint, I suppose.'

'Not the action of your average mugger, is it?'

'I suppose I humiliated him a bit, got the better of him. Packed him off with a flea in his ear.'

'Did you take anything that was his?'

'You're not taking it seriously? Christ, I don't believe it.'

Woolin spread his arms in a placatory manner across the wheel then, smiling.

'Listen,' he said, 'we're on the same side. You know I respect you, all of us do. Or most of us anyway. One of our officers, it seems, has talked to that newspaper reporter, too. Who've you been upsetting?'

'Nobody. Not that I can think of.'

It had occurred to me, that everybody seemed to have been talking to everybody else. Woolin had spoken to Sally, who'd spoken to Jo Hinchcliffe, who'd spoken to the mugger Ronald Pickles, who'd spoken to Chatterton. Was I being paranoid? I didn't think so at the time. Pickles, Hinchcliffe, Sally and Woolin. It seemed like more than coincidence, more than just me, James

Hartley Turner, who was binding it all together. I could no longer trust anyone, and I was certain of one thing: it had all started on that evening Ronald Pickles tried to mug me.

I picked up the keys to the car at the desk, wrote the cheque then and there, since it would doubtless bounce anyway, and Woolin walked me out to the compound.

'Tell me,' he boomed in the concrete underhall.

'Tell you what?'

'If nothing adds up, then something in the equation is crooked. Did you honestly say all that, about heroin and guns and sterilising the poor?'

His expression was a mixture of shocked amusement and pity.

'Not in so many words.'

'Did you and that reporter have something going?'

The question was one too many. It was still before nine in the morning and I'd had enough of the third degree.

'What do you want?'

He shrugged.

'Not to see you again. Not in anything other than your official capacity anyway.'

I climbed into the car. It had a peculiar sweet, musty smell.

Woolin knocked on the window.

'By the way,' he said, 'seems your friend left a calling card. I found that on the floor in your toilet.

He tossed the Jobseeker travel permit I'd taken from Ronald Pickles into my lap.

The remains of three joints were in the ash-tray. Roaches, paper and tobacco remains. This was obviously something the police hadn't overlooked. So why had they simply left them there and not said anything?

It didn't matter. They were simply confirmation now, of what a complete mug I'd been.

Twenty-four

'Ostman dat,' James Junior said.

'What?'

I could see Sally and her father through the window inside, on the sofa, watching television.

'Ostman dat, daddy.' James Junior said petulantly, stomping a foot on the silver lawn. He was only wearing a T-shirt and seemed oblivious to the cold.

'I'm glad you remember me,' I said.

'Ostman dat!' He turned and picked up a crimson tricycle, then kicked it over and came back.

'Look,' he said, gazing down into a rusted shrub at a glazed spider's web. I stooped down and we both inspected it from a distance of an inch, our frozen breath spiralling out together. 'Incy wincy out.'

He went over and kicked the tricycle again.

'Pointless being so petulantly pedantic,' I said.

He laughed then, and I wondered when the last time was, that anyone had laughed at anything I said. I held a hand out above the waist-high wall between us.

'Daddy, c'mon,' he tugged.

'Can't, son. Business to attend to.'

'Daddy, c'mon!' And he tilted his head back with adult concern, acquired from someone.

'You 'right?' he asked.

'I'm all right,' I said, after a few seconds. 'I have to see someone though now, urgently. Sort it all out.'

'Ostman dat.'

'And his black and white cat,' I replied, understanding. 'Yes indeed.'

I leaned over the wall, picked him up and kissed him, saw movement behind the window and put him down.

Back behind the wheel again, I was fast discovering the therapeutic pleasure of driving. I decided I wanted to do more of it then and there, without a destination, decided to get out of the city and really open the car up for an hour or so. After I'd seen Liz.

When I got to the mill, all the workers were huddled around, smoking and chatting in their overalls on the pavement. This was quite a common occurrence. Small fires were forever being caused by faulty bits of dilapidated equipment and the testing department's chemicals were still capable of giving off a cloud of something toxic and potentially damaging every few weeks, despite modern legislation.

Discovering my reserved space was occupied, I parked up in the visitors' section. I pushed my way through the bored-looking throng into the reception area. Two workmen were loading new-looking computer equipment back into boxes which dribbled polystyrene chips. Rolls of carpet were propped against the walls and executive chairs wrapped in plastic were acrobatically stacked in pairs.

'What's going on?' I asked the receptionist.

A picture of my father thundered accusations down from the wall behind her.

'Can I help you, sir?'

She was new, didn't know who I was.

'Get Liz for me, would you, tell her it's James.'

'I'm afraid Miss Armstrong isn't in at the moment.'

'Well, where is she?'

'I'm afraid she hasn't left details in the diary. We're trying to locate her. Can anyone else help?'

'Is Franklin in?'

'They're all in a meeting.'

'Well tell them it's James Hartley Turner.'

'I'm afraid I can't disturb them.'

Ignoring her protests, I barged through into what used to be my father's office. It was not how I remembered it. The gun metal filing cabinets were gone, and pieces of machinery were no longer spread on newspapers across lint-covered floorboards. Thick beige carpet lapped at apricot walls and there was the indefinable smell of a new car's interior.

Franklin and four sombre-suited men I didn't know were perched around what must have been Liz's work station, staring into the screen. They turned as I entered.

'Ah, gentlemen,' Franklin said, 'now here's someone who may be able to help us. Where's Liz, James? Can you shed any light?'

Twenty-five

After leaving the mill, my movements, for the record, were as follows:

Two miles out of Wakefield, I stopped at Heath Common, got out and walked across a farmer's field to survey the ruin there, which the historian had told me about. It was haunted, supposedly, by Lady Mary Bowles, who was said to be eternally troubled by her part in testifying to the devil possession of a witch, who'd been hanged at York. The ruin was covered in graffiti and littered with *Special Brew* cans and condoms. It was a bitterly cold but bright morning and the short walk left me breathless. I sat down on a worn-smooth slab, alert for any indication of mysterious atmosphere, deliberately concentrating on the wind and the slightest of movements, the most distant of sounds, to keep myself from thinking. A rustle in the undergrowth, probably a bird. Distant traffic. Nothing else.

How much thought do we waste on unresolved problems? Why do we feel the need to constantly re-run the unassailable events which lead to our personal predicaments? What did it matter now, that Lady Bowles had taken to her death bed with the curse of an old hag still resounding in her ears twenty years after her testimony?

I wanted my head entirely cleared of personal things, to vanish into the eternity of the landscape.

I headed then around the city for Walton Hall, the ancestral home of the Waterton family, and now a hotel and restaurant where Sally and I had dined with her parents on a number of occasions.

The 27th Lord of the place, Charles Waterton, was one of her father's favourite characters; an adventurer, eccentric, and keen taxidermist. A master at teasing hollows and protuberances into expressions of primate pleasure or pain. Inside the hall venomous snakes had once struck fearful poses, their forked tongues quivering and fangs erect. Others once lay coiled in harlequin folds, with dull gleaming eyes. Ant-bear and sloth, chimpanzee and cayman stared blankly on. Some examples of the Squire's handiwork were now in Wakefield Museum, along with a number of his more wayward creations, such as the Noctifer - part-gorget, part-eagle owl, and the Diabolus Bellicosus - a lizard blessed with abnormal horns and spikes. The balcony rails of Walton Hall had been a perch for myriad, exotically-plumed birds.

At some stage Waterton went deep into Guyana, where years earlier Sir Walter Raleigh had searched for the mythical gold of Eldorado. The purpose of the Squire's journey however, had been to collect the pure poison used by the indigenous Indians on their arrowheads, which he believed might have medicinal value. He travelled barefoot and without maps up the Demerara and Essequibo rivers, making contact with the Macusi Indians at a tributary called Apoura-poura.

Back at the London Veterinary College he stabbed three donkeys with poisoned wild-hog arrows and managed to bring one back from the dead with a pair of bellows down the windpipe. In this way, the commonly-used anaesthetic curare was introduced to modern medicine.

The donkey was called Wouralia, the historian had informed me, whispering the name with appreciation, and had lived for many years after its ordeal at Walton Hall.

From the hill opposite I stared down at the hall and the lake on which Squire Waterton's funeral pyre had been borne. The flower-bedecked craft bearing his body was tailed by hundreds of smaller boats.

I was trying, in my way, to make history come alive as a means of escape, to achieve that elsewhere contentedness I so envied in Sally's father. But all I really saw was trees and water.

I drove on, out to the village of Denby Dale, where they made giant pies to commemorate state occasions of note. A four-ton monster baked for Queen Victoria's Jubilee had to be prised from the oven by a dozen men using tram-lines as crow bars. Another of the historian's gems. Unfortunately the meat was not prime product and the pie was condemned and buried in quick lime.

I decided then - or perhaps the decision had already been made - to drive out to the moors and visit the farm which had formerly belonged to my father, and where I'd spent a good deal of my childhood. It had been some time since I'd ventured up that way and I was curious to know how the place was being managed these days.

The driving kept me from thinking. I was almost grateful at being blocked behind the meandering mobile homes, snailing tractors and overcautious pensioners at the wheels of spanking new Rovers. The anger these provoked, useless and ill-advised as it was, somehow made me feel better.

I stopped for lunch at a village pub along the way, in which the landlord and his solitary octogenarian regular held a conversation which seemed to me as ritually gnarled and pitted as the paint scarred stones of the ruin of Heath Hall. Neither listened to the words of the other. Each would now and then go over and fuss a tired old sheepdog in a basket under the dartboard. I started to quite envy too, such still, untroubled life. Perhaps when everything blew over...

Rain was performing a military tattoo on the car roof by the time I approached the farm, and through the sluices across the windscreen I only just caught the turn-off. Two hundred yards along the drive, in any case, the road was barred by a huge metal gate festooned with forbidding signs and warnings. The farm had been entirely walled by brickwork fringed with barbed wire, and the building I could see in the distance above it was unrecognisable, a fortress of white walls and stained double glazing. The old wooden cowsheds, barns and stables had been replaced with brick and aluminium constructions. Only the smell of the place was familiar as I got out of the car, the rain pounding up the pungency of cows and horses and sheep.

Despite having no umbrella I waded through mulched autumn leaves up to the bolted and padlocked gates. There was an intercom which I pressed, but it made no sound and nobody answered. Quite what I would have said in any case, I don't know. I started to walk around the wall, through the mud, wanting a closer look, thinking there must be a back entrance. There was barely a path, and I tripped on a couple of occasions. The rain became even heavier, but just as I decided to head back for the car, I noticed the indistinct shape of something man-made across a ploughed field.

It was still there. I reached the well first, down which Brian and I had dropped stones all those years ago. The winch and handle that had lowered and raised the bucket were long gone and the mouth was completely sealed with sodden bindweed.

Waist-high brambles and nettles partially blocked the old door of the crumbling building. I could just discern the faded letters AN painted above the frame. ANIMAL FEED and KINDLING, the message had once read. I walked around the side to a lean-to, and there it was under a tarpaulin sheet, the old sidecar. As the rain lashed down, my senses were filled with thirty-year old smells, diesel and creosote. Head down against the pummelling rain, I walked back to the door. I pushed, and it opened slightly, but something heavy was behind it. With my shoulder, I forced open a more amenable space, to discover a porcelain trough half-full of water. I stepped over this, inside. Half of the roof had fallen in and the rain had turned a left-behind carpet to pulp. Weeds sprouted through its spaces. The place bore all the tell-tale signs of being a haunt of local children - more discarded beer cans and the remains of a couple of small fires; supermarket carrier bags inexpertly tacked against the windows; an abandoned mattress pushed into a corner, doubtless the vehicle of prepubescent fumblings.

I lay down on this, and listened to the rain.

Twenty-six

The water was up to my neck and my body was heavy as lead with it, but the old woman still had flames coming off her arms. The fire had melted her face too, and the shrieks emanating from her mouth were tortured and relentless.

'It boils,
thou'll drink,
he'll speak,
thou'll think.'

Pipe clenched between his teeth, my father was forcing a pair of metal bellows down the throat of a mill worker in a corner, whilst in the back of the BMW Sally was in the throes of copulation with a feral boy whose buttocks gyrated provocatively in front of my face. Colin Chatterton, grinning as he toked on a joint before stubbing it out in the car's elongated ash-tray, then minced around the scene, drawing attention to each of its components with exaggerated hand gestures for my delectation. The malevolent eyes of a thousand court defendants stared down from the hole in the roof, illuminated by a shaft of light in which raindrops danced.

'Sign this,' Jo Hinchcliffe laughed, and danced coquettishly away from me.

'Come on then,' said Liz Armstrong, in her old uniform of green overalls, glasses taped to the side of her head.

'You don't know bugger all about shit,' Sergeant Dick Woolin told me, snarling from inside a rubber mask of Barney Rubble. 'Or that's what you want us to think.'

'All right, Daddy,' my son said, in that heart-aching imitation of adult concern. 'You all right?'

My dreams, I remember thinking at that moment - for I was aware I was dreaming - are not in the least bit creative, merely a tape of past events being scrambled as they are rewound.

'No I'm not,' I said, 'not at all, I'm afraid.'

And then the historian appeared, and smashed a pool cue over my head.

The crazed eyes staring into my own as I started awake, and the wet ropes of hair and the hands which were grabbing my shirt, were suddenly real.

Not yet awake, I tried to make sense of my surroundings while fending her off, but my initial attempt at an explanation came out all sleep-shaken and she fluttered and shrieked around me like a bird in a trap. My clothes were soaking and my back and legs were numb. Thick-headed, I allowed myself to be ushered from the stinking mattress and driven out into the darkness, where the relentless rain attempted to hammer me like a peg into the mud.

I tried to placate her, to explain who I was, what I was doing there, but she remained on the threshold, flashing a torch at me. I waved the letter at her, to no avail. Eventually I gave up, and felt the thin beam dancing on my shoulders as I trudged back to the car.

Christ, he had no idea, behind his bar on the other side of the world, that she'd come to this.

Or surely he'd have done something.

Twenty-seven

Back in Wakefield, late that evening, I drove up and down Westgate looking for them in the sea of faces, determined to get some answers, picking in a desultory fashion at the salad wrapped around a kebab spread in paper on my lap. Two bottles of vodka I'd bought from an off-licence with my remaining cash rolled about under the seats. Garlands of light zig-zagged across the road and the tribes moved from pub to pub. My clothes were clogged with mud and steaming under the blast of the car's heater. The rain had turned to sleet – snow on its way – but it might just as well have been mid July in Wakefield. Short skirts and bare arms were the order of the day, toeless shoes and tattoos. The police had their cars parked down a number of side streets. As I passed slowly, I looked into the vehicles for Woolin or Forrester. Occasionally I was taken for a taxi and giggling gangs jumped into the road, attempting to flag me down, spraying obscenities and aerosol snow across the windscreen.

There was an atmosphere of hysterical brotherhood on the streets. Modern drugs kicking in, and Slade's Xmas anthem bellowed out. 'Lager, lager, lager,' others chanted. People hugged and kissed and linked arms with a murderous shedding of their natural reticence which would end in tears, one way or another.

I finally abandoned the search and parked by The Wool Scourer, which would shortly be depositing its remaining clientele out onto the pavements.

Perhaps, if they were actually in there, they'd go on to a club. If so, I'd wait. All night if I had to.

The heart of the city, to the north, was still giving off a muted animal cacophony of raucous singing, erratic fireworks and shrieks. Sporadic football chants erupted, club music – all accelerated heartbeat drums and bass – pumped from the open doorways of pubs and clubs. Stiletto shoes slapped down the precinct to the west, car horns blared. But down the back street all was, for the moment, enclosed in the bubble of sleet and distance.

I closed my eyes and I could see the old woman's face above me again, the bulging eyes full of animal fear, the seaweed slaps of her hair as she pulled me from the dream and attempted to remove me from her bed, black nails flashing.

The door of the pub opened, throwing a dagger of light in my direction. A group of men in shirt-sleeves moved with apparent determination directly towards the car, and then melted around it as if it were invisible, meandering between the bare market stall frames. I threw the remains of the kebab out of the window after them. Two girls carrying a third between their shoulders came out next, lurching in the general direction of the taxi rank. More men with monstrous guts and facial hair then, cue-cases over their shoulders like guns, and I almost missed him as he ducked around the side of the building. I knew it led nowhere, and thirty seconds later he re-emerged, zipping up his flies and burping. He was alone and I let him amble two hundred yards with beery carelessness before getting out of the car.

He was heading home, I realised, as he descended into the precinct under the dual carriageway. I had his address, of course, from the files. It was the first place I'd stopped, but there was nobody home. A blanket over the window, and a pile of old vegetable boxes by the door.

I let him reappear at the other side before skipping over the metal protective barrier at road level, darting across the carriageway as he turned a corner. As I got to this I saw that he'd stopped to talk to someone, and I hovered rather ridiculously by a bush until I heard other people approaching from behind. Pretending to be seeking an imaginary dog and momentarily experiencing a rush of nerves as I feared ambush, I let the middle-aged group of good-natured revellers pass.

'Looks like bleeding Worzel Gummidge,' a woman said, and they all laughed without malice. No offence intended or taken.

I listened to their footsteps recede before turning the corner. Pickles was inside his house now.

I got to his door and saw the thin light coming from under the blanket. I went around the back where wheely-bins were overturned and cats truffled as they howled. Bike-frames and punctured soccer balls. I eventually located the right house, snaked along the path and peered in through the kitchen window.

And then I heard the music – faltering stabs at the first line of a familiar melody played over and over again. On a clarinet. *Stranger on the Shore*, I think it was supposed to be. The door opened and Pickles stood there, his fist gripping the silver keys of one of my father's black instruments. Our eyes met, but I felt nothing of that certainty, that indignation and righteousness, I'd experienced on our first meeting, outside my own door. I had no desire to be John Wayne this time. I was simply too tired, but I was able to imagine a vague *film noir* scenario in which, as ruthless inquisitor, I burned cigarettes on a bound Ronald, who squinted into blinding light and eventually told me things I wanted to know.

'I've got a couple of these,' he said, raising the clarinet, 'so I thought I should learn to play it. Too fussy, though. Made for girls' fingers.'

'Like Acker Bilk?' I said.

'What?'

He jutted his chin forward, as if sensing I was making fun of him, and I seized the opportunity to capitalise on his ignorance.

'Most concert pianists, I think you'll find, have rather deceptively podgy and ungraceful fingers, much like your own. Mozart was no exception, apparently.'

'Fuck right off,' he sneered.

'But aren't you worried that they might constitute evidence, anyway?' I continued quickly, gesturing at the clarinet in his hands.

He tilted his head to one side, considering this, before reaching a conclusion which registered on his face like a light bulb pinging on in a cartoon thought bubble.

'Nah. No chance.'

'Why not? Remember who you're dealing with. I have friends in all the right places.'

He took a step forward out from the doorway and thrust the clarinet at me.

'Did you like the story in the paper?'

'Not particularly.'

'I think she's got you sussed, that bird. Look at you,' he said. 'Right fuckin' state. Pigs'll be here in a minute, and you're on private property. Col Chatterton's given me his professional advice for nothing and all. Gratis. Says to take out an injunction. Which I might. And I'll get Legal Aid.'

I dashed at him then, rather wearily, and only half-heartedly expecting something glamorous to be the result, clinging on to him as if I were drowning.

I got the bell of my father's old clarinet across the bridge of my nose for my trouble. And God, it hurt. Eyes watering, I stumbled forward and lost my balance. In which time Pickles had slammed the door and locked it behind him.

I shouted and hammered on the door from the ground, then, defeated, rolled back against the wall and contemplated the empty sky.

After about a minute the letterbox creaked slyly open.

'Are you still there?' Pickles whispered through it. 'I know you are. Just fuck off will you. Or don't. Wait for them to cart you off. See if you like it in the cells.'

'I've figured it out,' I said.

'Well done, Sherlock.'

'Ansell Simmonds is the fence, isn't he, saw things he wanted?'

'Might be. Drew the line at shitty old clarinets, though, didn't he? Why should I tell you anything? Then again, what the fuck does it matter? You can't touch us now. If you ever could, that is.'

'I wouldn't be so sure.'

'Stay there then.'

'You were casing the place, that first time, weren't you?'

'Jimmy was round the corner, you know. Lucky for you he didn't decide to steam in, but I was a bit pissed off when he didn't. Supposed to be a mate, and always mad for it.'

'So you came back.'

'Course we came back. Like sleeping dogs.'

'I think you'll find they're supposed to just lie.'

There was a pause, as Ronald tried to fathom this remark.

'Cleaned you out, didn't we?' he said, finally.

'It didn't connect at the time,' I told him. 'Of course you were there that night.'

There was laughter from behind the door.

'There you were sleeping like a baby with all that booze inside you, Mister Turner, after all the shouting and carrying on. You killed Kevin, she kept shouting. Who, we wondered, was this Kevin?'

'Just a dog.'

'We were thinking blackmail, at first. Why not? If you were a murderer?'

'So there you were, on my property again.'

'We like the little villages, when we're in wandering moods.'

'Just tell me what happened.'

'I don't see that I owe you any explanations, but like I said, there was all that shouting about murder, and then your wife tramping off with the ankle-snapper to shit knows where and leaving the door wide open. Well it was too much of an opportunity. You spoilt the surprise, of course, by barely registering a pulse there, head down in all them papers, with your mouth open like a drain.'

Mysterious bumping and banging in my deep, disturbed sleep.

'So we thought we might as well rob you anyway,' Pickles continued. 'Piled half of it into your car, all the furniture, smashed some of it up to fit. It turned into a competition between the two of us. What a wheeze. Jimmy had his pick-up and we loaded that up too. He's a piranha, I'm fucking telling you. Mad for it all. Wanted to strip the floorboards and would have done the roof too, if we hadn't both been so skunked. Said we should bury you in the garden. Who'd know? God, it was a laugh. You should have been there. Not that we got much for our trouble.'

So, as I had come to realise over the last couple of days, no Sally and lover, furtively stripping the place between kisses as I'd imagined, instead Pickles and Raven, brazenly violating my space as I slumped there, unconscious. I was grateful to Ronald for this confirmation, and undid the flies to my mud-spattered trousers then and there.

'And you never even realised you'd been done did you?' he continued. 'Well they won't believe you now, after all that...'

The sure jet put an end to his soliloquy.

'Bastard!' Ronald howled.

It was fitting somehow, a gesture of my forgiveness. What was actually taking place, was that old class thing again. There was I, privileged, educated, his natural superior, demanding what I knew I was entitled to, namely his respect and obedience.

Pissing through a letterbox.

A car had pulled up at the front of his house and someone was knocking at his door. The situation, I was aware, would strike a further blow to my near-devastated career and reputation.

Twenty-eight

No alarm bell rang and no Rottweiler bounded out of the shadows as the french window frame strained and splintered, before its glass finally shattered. Shards danced around me on the shingled drive. I pulled the bottle of vodka from the waist of my trousers and took a long gulp, feeling the molten liquid falling through my chest.

She wasn't in. I remembered what Sally had said, about the move.

I hovered there on the edge of an expanse of cream carpet, mottled with craters where the legs of heavy furniture had recently stood.

An image of scrolled claws and piano keys was conjured by the memory of wood polish. A huge Cheese Plant drooped from a pot in the corner, leaves nibbled paler at the edges, an upturned telephone snaking out from under it. I had an image of Sally sitting cross-legged beside it, pouring out her troubles to Liz. I listened to the air swooning up from my lungs, strained for raised voices, switches suddenly sprung and any other sound of nearby activity, finally locating only the meshing gears of a far-off train. The central heating system gurgled and a flock of birds fluttered in my chest.

I paced across the milky shadow-pile and pulled at a door handle. The kitchen, though unlit, was clearly a shell, its racks empty, wall units gaping open. The light flickered as I pushed the switch, tantalising me with strobe glimpses of pine and marbled surfaces before finally flooding the room.

There was a wrapped Christmas tree perched in the corner. In the washing-up bowl, a plastic colander, melted around half its rim. Under the sink, rags and shoe polish, plastic pegs and florets of cloth. In an overhead cupboard, three tins of *Heinz* ravioli, a leaking white sachet of powdered soup and a pile of unopened mail.

The top letter was addressed to myself at the mill.

Dear Sir,
I write to inform you that, in view of your refusal to respond to our previous letters,

The second was for Liz, but I opened it anyway.

Dear Miss Armstrong,
In view of the recent correspondence in respect of matters of which you are well aware, we have been forced to inform our solicitor to...

So Sally's intuition was bang on the nail and old Franklin's fears were grounded in fact. Taking the letters with me, I moved into the hall and decided to inspect upstairs. Nothing at all of any interest: the skeleton of a bed, a pair of stepladders, a clutter of abandoned aerosols in the bathroom.

I tore open more of the letters. Demands in buff envelopes, invoices, red reminders, final demands. Split fifty-fifty between myself and Liz.

I was half way down the stairs again, when the noise registered. How long it had been there I couldn't say, but I froze when I recognised it. A car was pulling up outside. The headlights danced from a bedroom window above me. Suddenly, footsteps were crunching up to the front door. I crouched down out of view as a key turned in the lock. Coat buttoned to her throat, Liz turned the light on and within seconds had started to climb the stairs. She had her head down and was adjusting the strap of her watch, so that when she finally looked up, she was almost on top of me and gasped with the shock.

'Jesus!' She stopped dead, breathing heavily. 'What the hell are you doing? Christ, you nearly frightened me to death. What are you doing in my house?'

There seemed little I could say to this. She leaned against the bannister rail.

'You'd better leave right now or I'll call the police.'

Everybody, suddenly, was threatening me with the police.

'You won't do that.'

'Sally said you were acting strangely.'

Everybody, suddenly, was judging me.

'I'm not the only one.'

'You were a bastard to her, Turner. She didn't deserve it. That poor dog. Have you thought about what impression it's making on that beautiful child of yours?'

'I'm not here to talk about my wife, or my son.'

I had no control over my voice anymore. Barks were whispers, exclamations came out as questions.

'God, I'm shaking.' She sat on the stairs below me and caught her breath, finally looking up at me. 'What's happened to you, Turner? Look at the state of you.'

'I called at the mill this morning. They want to know where you are.'

'God, your clothes. When was the last time you washed?'

'I left a message for you to contact me.'

'I've been busy.'

She unbuttoned her coat and took out a handkerchief, dabbing first her lipstick and then her forehead. A pearl smear above her left eye.

'You've sunk things,' I said.

'I don't doubt you'd like them to try and blame it all on me now.'

She looked up at me. Her eyes were clouding with tears. How genuine they were was another matter.

'Don't bother with the act for my benefit,' I said. 'I never had you figured for the emotional type.'

Her head darted back down and she dabbed at her eyes.

'You never had much figured at all, did you? And anyway, fuck you.'

'You're leaving, aren't you?'

'I have to, now,' she sniffed.

'What about these,' I said, waving the wad of letters at her. 'Shouldn't you take them?'

'Yes, I suppose I should.' She smiled.

I flourished the letters above my head.

'Carry the ball and run with it,' I said. 'Isn't that what you told Sally to do? Pretend you're playing for the team, but don't pass?'

She shook her head sadly. I put the letters down on the carpet.

'Clogs to clogs...' she murmured, moving sideways to gaze down the stairs, so that we were no longer uncomfortably face to face. 'That's what they say, isn't it? 'Clogs to clogs in three generations.' Your grandfather started it all...'

'I never knew him,' I said. 'Died when I was two.'

'Whatever...'

Gingerly, she extended an arm. I caught a waft of her perfume, then held her hand, rubbing my thumb along the knuckle of her index finger. It was as dry and brittle as paper, but warm.

'Your father took it to the limit,' she continued, 'and now you...'

'And you,' I added.

We remained there for several minutes, survivors of something beyond our grasp, and recognising it.

'I was his prostitute,' she said, eventually. 'That's what it amounts to. They can pore over the books now, but they won't find any of that itemised.'

I allowed my eyes to close, and tried to imagine total silence. It cannot exist, I realised. There was a buzzing, a roaring in my ears. The rumble and gurgle of close-by appliances, water through pipes, gas and electricity on stand-by. Prone bodies in the beds of adjacent buildings, inhaling and exhaling. The razor swish of far-off transport systems, trains and taxis and cars. The planet perambulating on its axis. The creak of its satellites and the slow orbit of the sun and stars.

I could sense Liz stiffening as she received no reply, no longer able to see my face, to gauge my reaction.

'What price all that personal attention,' she asked uncertainly, 'those little favours for our clients? They closed the deals, kept things moving. Do you think I enjoyed it? I did it because it was necessary. I was out in the real world and your father, my pimp, never even had to leave his office.'

She was weeping again, silently to herself. I moved down a step and put my arm around her shoulder. However inappropriate, I wanted to somehow comfort her. The tears of a woman - real or otherwise - fly in the face of every instinct for self-preservation; batter down the walls of rational thought as if they were soggy paper.

I licked a finger and removed the lipstick smudge from above her eye. I stroked her hair.

'And after that,' she said, brightening, 'I was on my own.'

I inched the bottle of vodka from the waist of my trousers, pulled off the top and took a gulp, then passed it forward to her.

'How did it start?'

I felt her swallow from the bottle.

'How it started is...' She took another drink. 'Just little things. Things you let slide and think you'll be able to catch up on afterwards. And things you know nobody will spot, or have the gumption to do anything about.'

'Like using my name, for instance?' I suggested.

She shook her head with annoyance.

'You allowed that to happen.' She turned to look at me again. 'When your father was there, well, nothing really escaped him. Put it that way. But even so, there's nothing to say he wouldn't have made the same mistakes I have recently.'

'You're joking,' I said, but her expression said otherwise.

'Things have changed, Turner. There's an element of risk to everything. His generation was the last to enjoy that stability, and he's lucky he didn't have to deal with it any other way. You should know what it's like.' Her eyes told me my empathy was immaterial. 'But give me credit where it's due. Things were going wrong in any case. We had a couple of years left at the most. It was obvious we had to find ways of adding value to what we were producing, tap into a few niche markets. Obvious to me, at least.'

'I had to send out the right signals to the industry,' she said, ambiguously. 'Keep up appearances.'

'You've been putting orders through for stock which has never arrived, haven't you?'

She passed me the bottle back as she got to her feet. She was smiling now.

'Why don't you try and prove that?' she suggested. 'I'm sure they'd like to hear that coming from you. You might find it a little hard to be convincing.'

'And what you have ordered recently, hasn't been paid for at all.'

'I think you'll find that's your problem.'

She gripped the bannister with one hand, still smiling.

I let out a low whistle, to emphasise my recognition of this predicament.

'It would have happened anyway,' she said. 'sooner or later. I'm not coming out of this in front, if that's what you're thinking. Not in the long term.'

'And you expect me to believe that?'

I put the bottle down at my side.

'Believe whatever you like,' she said. 'I've never been stupid, James, and these days I'm nobody's whore.'

Her expression was defiant.

'I'd better take those,' she said, gesturing towards the letters with a flutter of upturned fingers. A spider on its back.

And then she was gone.

Twenty-nine

Christmas day. Sally and her mother, their cheeks flushed with early drinks, would be greasing trays and dishes, the kitchen's windows sheened over with steam, its every available work surface groaning with produce, pans bubbling. The historian would be buried in a book, or perhaps playing with his grandchildren in a dug-out of torn paper and bright plastic, with my son, the youngest, tagging along at the heels of his cousins - Alan's litter of runts. The tree would dwarf the room, throw it into shadow. The steam would fill the house. Alan and his wife would have taken the opportunity to escape to the pub. On previous years, I had gratefully joined them.

It's a time for families and they all had them, the magistrates and the police officers, solicitors and journalists and thieves. They had their home comforts, the open fires, full bellies, pine-needled carpets, whisky glows. All other business had been postponed in the land of cheer and plenty.

And there was snow too, to make it all perfect. In the clear night I stared up as the moon's scrapings floated in, gently settling on my eyes. It had coated the trees and fields and the wind was bulldozing it up against the walls. It wasn't cold, too still, too gentle for that.

But Santa did not find me and Mrs Bennet. His reindeer must have sped by oblivious.

I had slept in my overcoat for three nights, the first two of them in the car. But on the third she'd said, 'Best keep in.' I finally had her trust, it seemed. She had cloth wrapped around her hands, newspaper stuffed into her clothes. We drank a sour apple mash that singed my insides and pressed against my temples, but still I replenished my cup from the clogged pot where it stewed. It didn't seem to affect her, but had doubtless contributed to her condition. She peered like a mole and shook even as she was carrying out some delicate operation with a needle and twine, lacing a ribbon around the tiny fir tree I uprooted by the stream and brought back with its roots still dangling. Sprigs of holly, too, but nothing to hang them on. Later we split the litre of *White Lightning* the village storekeeper, in a spasm of festive resignation, allowed her to stow under her folds, before prodding her out onto the pavement with his broom.

The inexpertly plucked moorhen and the mangled rabbit were charring on the radiator grill of an old car over the fire. Both had been found tyre-trodden and bloody out on the main road. Her fifteen meticulous, complicated traps had yielded nothing but small, inedible creatures - mice and sparrows. Beaten tin can constructions the traps, with fishgut gallows, bramble and strimmer twine lariats, rusty razor blade guillotines. She'd taken me on a tour of them all the day before, not because it was Christmas Eve, though I'd reminded her more than once, but because she could smell the snow coming. Deep into the woods, at the back of the farm, we scrabbled under festering moss canopies and leaf-mould nets, squinting into flinty holes for startled eyes and the silk of blood on her wires. She had a gun too, which she packed with mud. It couldn't do much but stun, but in those few essential seconds she could have been on her prey with a certainty which belied her arthritic, trembling demeanour. No timid cub-minder, this.

They threw out their surplus where she set her traps: supermarket bags full of flattened cans and privet cuttings, polystyrene packaging and defunct white goods; obstacle courses for the tiny animals to negotiate, once coaxed from holes and deep shadow.

She spat on the meat and poked the fire with the snub of the weapon, sending black smoke billowing up out of the roof. Staring at the long-blank television screen, her eyes jumped to non existent images.

'Told him,' she said, 'said it 'til I'm blue in the face, you've got to stand up to him.'

Sometimes she imagined me to be Brian, on other occasions her husband. I wanted to know what had happened to Mr Bennet, for he was surely dead. Not the type to leave her to this. I read her the letter too, from Australia, but wasn't sure if she understood its significance.

When Brian and I were growing up, the walls of the place, squalid as it was even then, had been smooth-plastered and papered, the roof pitched and sealed. Light filled the two rooms. Tidy. Simple and tidy. A portable generator had pumped life into a television set, the small fridge and the record player, those symbols of affluence and well-being. Nevertheless, they took their water from a drum under the gutter and their waste to the fields. But that was a long time ago.

Now, all was neglect and ruin. When it became a little warmer, I'd carry out a few essential repairs, do what I could for her, I decided. Not that she needed any looking after.

'I don't envy you one jot,' she said, though not actually to me as such, 'bide on that. You can keep your high ceilings and your full pantry and all them acres for what we all care. All that'll give you cankers, rot your insides and line and stoop you. Turn you grey and shrivelled, your heart too. Devil steals your milk, right enough. Can't do nothing about that.'

She let the meat burn, but we didn't taste it anyway, just ate to be eating. The guts and fur and feathers lay around our feet, downy blood clusters. And I was forgetting things. Allowing myself to forget already.

'Child, sweet child,' she said, on a separate occasion, 'you've got his hair, but who knows how? Must have been some red in my line, way back. All I pray is you have a bit of his heart too, and not all the other, all stone and blackness. And him, he'd pace about then, all at sixes and sevens, coughing that old cough from the dust, shitting himself but still wanting to do the right thing, even if he'd never stand up to him. Too much heart, but kind heart never got to king of the castle.'

'Never king of the castle,' I'd agree.

She was only coherent about the past and then it was as if the carpet still had its lustre, the television was still a flickering pantheon and they'd be coming back at any time, father and son, one on the bike, the other in the rickety sidecar. And she was sewing a dress, of sequins and tassels, with cloth that had been given to her.

Had I not wished to remain in hiding, I could surely have got to the bottom of her story. The locals doubtless all knew Mad Jane Bennet. Some pitied her, leaving their leftovers and cast-offs at her door. Others feared or despised her. A couple of hundred years ago she'd have scratched a living selling potions and cures, until they decided to burn her. But she kept herself to herself mostly, unless she was in a stealing frame of mind. They were certainly unaware she had a visitor for the Christmas season, and perhaps longer.

Because there was really nowhere else I could think to go, unwelcome as I was.

I got home the night after I saw Liz, to find strangers waiting at the door, anxious to present me with a piece of paper. Gave them the keys and got back in the car. When your luck's out, there's no point in fighting it. Merry Christmas.

Thirty

Vague memories were stirring, of the stories Mrs Bennet told me and Brian as children. Now however, the comic characters who'd populated them had been transformed into narrow, drunken grotesques.

There was her father, with his love of the belt, chasing her round the kitchen. Chickens fenced in with wire under the table, pecking at the suds from stout bottles.

'Big belt,' Jane said, dreamily, 'like a weight-lifter's, and nothing really to hold up.'

'A proud man, though?' I suggested, at which she narrowed her eyes shrewdly, suddenly lucid.

'Pride's what you have for falling through the holes in your pockets. Coal scrapings in a tin bath.'

Too much spit, she said, at the corners of his mean mouth, like a sheep with the dropsy.

I pictured him sinking gratefully into his armchair, like a punctured football, having administered a beating. Tyrant though my own father may have been, he was at least in control, and able to provide for his family.

Then there was the village priest, and the sisters with their straps and rosaries and scrubbing brushes, who also played their part in finally driving her across the water to Liverpool. Where she met Frank.

Kind Frank, no boozer, who queued at the sheeting works most mornings, and if he was lucky would come back with his clothes coated in dust and a day's wages in his pocket. And still read comics, *The Hotspur* and *The Dandy*, like a big kid.

'Gave him that cough working there, what else would do it? He put the roof over my head, and I was more than in his debt, but then his own kin dies and we had to meet the rent. Met it head-on. Wouldn't let me make ends meet the natural way, and no harm in it when you're desperate. Far too proud for that. Pride's got a big belt holding bugger all up. But the landlord's henchmen chased us out with knives and dogs, burst in the night and had us on our way, like tinkers, clothes on our backs was about the size of that, a few sticks, what we could carry. And I was never a towny anyhow, with a yearning for open and the air and something to smell but soot and shit, get that silt off your chest it will.'

And so, it seems, they moved inland, and Frank eventually found work on my father's farm.

'More or less a second string to the bow, all that land, what with owning a mill too, and houses; I said to him, Frank, we'll be in clover, won't be there breathing down your back from noon to dusk. Not all the time anyway. Likely as not preoccupied. Little did I know. But a place to live, with that being part of the terms. And he knew Frank were weak, and that dare say suited him.'

Boxing Day morning, as I was pulling clumps of frozen bindweed from the old well, having broken its seal of ice, we heard the master of the local hunt's horn in the distance.

I was dreaming of restoring the place to its former glory. I'd mend the roof, pitch and seal. Dig the ground around the place, once it thawed, plant seeds. FRESH VEG and KINDLING would be repainted in bold letters across the front of the cottage. And the fresh vegetables would be tended by me. I'd watch the shoots pushing out of the earth as I chopped logs. It wasn't much to ask.

Half an hour later, the horn sounded again, closer, and Jane beckoned me inside.

Five minutes again, and the dogs skidded and thundered on the snow up to the brickwork, pushing their liverish tongues through the slats. Jane flicked the holly at their wet noses, making them yelp. Riders followed, thundering up and dismounting. Somebody rattled the door.

'It's Mad Jane's place,' another shouted.

'You got our fox in there you old crone?'

'They'll smell her above any vermin.'

'She'll put a curse on you boy, then you'll know 'bout it.'

'She'll be unconscious more like it. Sleeping off what she stole from my shop.'

The dogs howled with outrage as they were dragged and kicked into line, and were off again, the horn blaring as I threw open the door.

The huntsmen just stared at me. Some perhaps thought they vaguely recognised me, but of course couldn't place me here in this context, and after so many years. Mistletoe in helmet straps, tilting at hip-flasks. Warily they turned the horses and I watched the hooves kicking up the snow, polished boots digging into glossy flanks as they set off at a trot, a few of them unable to resist glancing back, before the scarlet backs were bobbing off to the horizon, across the zebra-striped fields.

'God knows I knew enough about what he was up to behind that poor woman's back all right,' Jane said, back inside. 'First hand. Titted that poor bugger's own for her half the time, and his kin. Both from the same seed.'

My head throbbed with what we'd drunk the previous day and what I was still having to acknowledge. I ached to be clean, suddenly plagued by itching, imagining insects under my suit.

'I was a handsome woman,' she said, 'a full woman, with a bit more blood running through my veins than her, up in that big draughty house, skivvying and prone in any case. And she'd knock on this door at any hour of the night, at her wit's end and in her night clothes, the bairn in her arms, wet-through sometimes, wide-eyed and all nettled and grazed.'

'See, she didn't have goodness in her, not in that way. I don't know about where she came from, what they fed her on there, but she was too weak herself, too much like a child. And she couldn't talk about nothing apart from him, that was all that mattered, and that's why she put up with it, I reckon. You might start off loving the husband - though I doubt she ever did - but then you get the son, and he's what counts. And the husbands just keep on being like sons, only bigger and more dangerous, but they don't get it back anymore. And they can be tall as trees and strong as oxes, but they won't ever get what they want again. Not really.'

'And him, my Frank, he was another kid - this gun, he'd cower and cry rather than point it the right way - but when he knew it was going to happen, knew it had happened and nothing he could do - you know what I'm talking about Brian, don't you?'

'I'm not Brian, Jane. It's James. But Brian's all right. That's why he wanted me to come.'

She refused to register this, carried on.

'He'd pace about then, all at sixes and sevens, coughing that cough, shitting himself but still wanting to do the right thing, even if he'd never stand up to him. But the gaffer never came those times. He'd only turn up when he'd got my Frank well out of the way, on another wild goose chase errand, and her too exhausted inside to raise a whisper. That's how it were done. My Brian.'

'His hair, though, thank God, is Frank's, and hopefully his heart too. But if that's it then so where is he?'

Thirty-one

Days passed, and I was happy to let them. You forget, given half the opportunity, think that because you're out of sight you're out of mind. But that's never the case at all. You're in a tray somewhere, the sheets of paper gradually shuffle until you're on the top, and immediate action is finally necessary. It is not possible to lurk, on paper, nor to cover your tracks.

Jane could exist because there was no paper to flutter after her. She did not crop up in columns and ledgers, and therefore there was no reason to act on her paperwork. Some might say she was lucky; others would class her as lost. Most would have no reason to class her at all. The things she ate and drank were not itemised on supermarket check-out chits, she was not a utilities subscriber, nor did the machinations of the state impinge. Her movements were not taxed, superannuated and solidified.

All those years ago, it never struck me that when I was Tom Sawyer to her son Brian's Huck Finn, I was adopting a mantel of which he would always be free.

They would never care about Brian, wherever he might be. But they would come back for me, because my movements were recorded. How could I simply disappear, with so much time and paper invested in my existence?

They came in the dead of night, beating back the bracken as they pushed down her door, poking the torches into our faces and uttering exclamations of disgust at what the beams revealed. The days had passed, and as Christmas receded I really started to believe I was forgotten, that they'd lost me.

'Rutted me like a bull,' she'd said, 'when he knew they were all out of the way, Frank probably reading a comic in some hidey hole. I was an attractive woman still. Pushed and shoved like he'd never do with her.'

A shaft from a torch caught the coiled grass snakes in a bucket, feeding on young spawn. It made them gasp. Stunned with mud pellets from the wheezing chamber, and snatched and tugged from the snowy banks. They put their hands over their mouths, coughing and gagging.

'Did it different with the hired help, like they had no feelings. And then later, would have taken the stick to him, and Brian, like they were nothing.'

Their shoes melting into the saturated carpet and the smell of our two unwashed bodies and burst mould spores.

'And that's how I fell with Brian. But he never had his hair.'

They tipped out the still quite unnecessarily and threw various items out onto the snow-patched grass, traps and beer cans, the mattress from under her, the old and useless television set. The huntsmen had alerted them, it seems, and quite separately the car had been found. Out in the country, nothing is private, everybody knows everybody's business. Jane Bennet made a near-maternal song and dance, spitting at them and cursing under the moon as they put me in their car.

'Just once,' she'd said, 'I thought he was going to blurt it all out, make a clean breast of it, though where that would leave us... Christmas it was, invited us up to see how the other half lived, gave Brian a better present than yon Lord Fauntleroy who I'd taken to my own breast for fear he'd waste. Posh watch, it were too.'

Outside the police station somebody took a photograph, a blinding flash which caught me full in the face. This annoyed the men I was with. Inside they let me take a shower and gave me a clean white T-shirt and a pair of oversized jogging pants. Nobody said much. Somewhere down below a man was shouting his lungs out, kicking and rattling a door.

'Batteries are running down,' somebody said.

The light was poor, corridors half-lit by solitary bulbs making a muted throb, contributing to an atmosphere, save for the shouter, of turpitude and resignation. In the cell the rays hardly penetrated under the door, but I slept solidly enough.

In the morning the light was barely any better, but the new shift was chirpier, and they were obviously amused by me.

'Here we are Catweazle,' a beaming oaf chirped as he entered with tea and toast, 'get that down you. Make a change from dandelion leaves, eh? Said it would make you heave, that place you were sleeping in.'

A barber appeared from somewhere - surely he wasn't a regular fixture - and gave me a shave. 'Let's get that face fuzz sorted out shall we?' Whistling as he frothed and making comments about the weather.

And then, in another room, across a bare desk, the questions started. Clean-cut college types, my inquisitors, an impeccable pair of suits who never raised their voices, quick-witted enough underneath the inscrutable exteriors, not about to miss anything. The preliminaries: Do you want a solicitor? Hardly. Is there anyone you'd like to phone? No. Will you talk to us openly? Shrug, nothing to hide. Tape rolling.

I told them everything I thought they wanted to know, volunteering more than was perhaps wise, but they seemed to take little interest in the finer details. They were not interested in Ronald Pickles, the story that appeared in the local newspaper, Colin Chatterton's accusations. Instead they pressed me again and again about Liz Armstrong, when had I last seen her, how long had I known her. I started to try and explain, as best I could, about my half-brother Brian, my father's dark secret. But they cut me short and showed me a series of specimen signatures, my own, and those of Armstrong, anxious that I should confirm the authenticity of each. Asked me about specific dates and times and figures.

You're not telling us anything we want to know here, they said. You're holding back, trying to pull the wool over our eyes. Tape clicked off.

They left, they came back.

Liz Armstrong. She worked first for your father. How long ago was that? And when he died, you took the helm and she did the work. Sleeping MD? But you were hardly that, were you? Everything passed through your hands, required your endorsement. When did you say you last saw her? You were pretty close then? Dates and times and figures, and account numbers. On and on, and then another exit, heads shaking in disappointment this time.

Back again, with renewed vigour, an edge to the even voices. Accusations.

We've spoken to your wife, and though she confirms your story, you haven't given us the impression they were so close. So that last time, she visited you. And that was unusual, was it? That was the first time she'd been to your house, and the last time you saw her? You see, we find that a little hard to believe. She left papers for you to examine. And you signed cheques for her. And she got drunk with your wife, that's correct? Your wife says she told you about her own misgivings, yet you did nothing about it.

It's only your view that she's left the country, they said. Her car was found outside her house. Why would she leave it there? And someone had forced entry.

I countered with the fact that her furniture had all been placed in storage, and they changed tack.

We don't know how you sleep at night, anyway, with all of it on your conscience, if you have one. There are a lot of people, angry people, who'd like some explanation. Answers. What kind of Christmas d'you think theirs has been? The honest workers, they're the ones who are suffering because of what you've done, wondering what kind of future faces them. The state certainly doesn't take kindly to this kind of thing.

Whose idea was it in the first place, hers or yours? Did you start to get yourself out of some kind of trouble? And then find it all too easy just to continue, become more brazen about it when it seemed nobody was going to find out?

Dates and times and figures and account numbers. I had no idea what they were all amounting to.

Thirty-two

Jane is in her new flat, pouring tea from a brown pot. She wears a padded waistcoat over a tracksuit and her hair has been hacked and coaxed into tight curls. We see a picture of a man and a boy in a frame on the table.

'Would you like a biscuit?' she says.

The light is bad and the man with the hand-held camera trails her into a booth-like kitchen. He appears to have to stoop at the threshold, scanning a stretch of chequered lino, a box of coal, a bag of potatoes.

Next she's shown walking in the park, seeming neither unaware of the camera, nor concerned by it. The music is of the type usually reserved for soft focus wedding shots in soap operas. I'm reminded of a documentary I saw, of a group of Kalahari Bushmen, forced through hardship onto a missionary reservation. The film crew make Jane sit on a swing in the children's playground, where she grins inanely as canned applause obliterates the music and the show returns to the studio.

Jo Hinchcliffe smiles out from a huge violet sofa, Jane at her side, squinting into the lights and wearing the same costume as in the earlier clips. Jo's former co-presenter is no longer on the show.

'Well Jane,' she says, 'it's been an extraordinary year for you hasn't it?'

'Yar,' Jane agrees, her attention fixed on some point in the middle distance.

'And it all started last Christmas, didn't it, when you had a visitor. Can you remember who that was?'

'Yar.'

The screen fills with the photograph of me taken outside the police station in which, with a thick black beard and engrimed clothes, I stare wildly, pointing a crooked, accusatory finger. This image has become familiar to the public.

'There he is,' Trevor said, twirling his key fob at my side, 'the man himself. Fame at last, eh?'

The photo was plastered across the regional newspapers - even made a couple of the nationals - when they picked me up.

'It was James Hartley Turner wasn't it, who used to own the farm next to where you lived?' The camera zooms in on Jo. 'Mr Turner is currently being detained at her majesty's pleasure pending investigations into the mismanagement of funds relating to the company founded by his father, Turner Mills, in Wakefield. The business was forced to close at the time, with the loss of 56 local jobs. Mystery still surrounds the circumstances of the case, and the police have been unsuccessful, to date, in tracing a Miss Liz Armstrong, who is also alleged to be involved. Mr Turner and others believe she may have fled the country. Well Jane, can you remember what he wanted?'

The camera pulls back and Jane shakes her head.

'Nar.'

'Whatever Mr Turner's motives in visiting Jane Bennet before finally being located by the police, the circumstances did serve to draw attention to the tragic circumstances to which Jane had been reduced. This was where she was living.'

A shot of the door of the crumbling cottage, waist-high nettles, then inside, lingering on the mattress and rubbish, sweeping up to the blocked-out windows and fixing on the torn roof.

Jo's voice-over: 'When her husband died four years ago, Jane had nobody to turn to and no source of income. Ignored by the social services, she retreated into herself, surviving by what the local people gave her.'

Back to the studio.

'Well Jane, I think it's fair to say you were at rock bottom weren't you? But now all that's changed, hasn't it?'

'Yar.'

'You've got a new place to live, with people close by to look after you. Are you happy?'

'Yar.'

'Well Jane, there's one more thing we think would make that happiness complete. You have a son, haven't you?'

Jane nods obligingly.

'Our Brian.'

'But you haven't seen him for many years now.'

'Had Frank's hair,' Jane said, shaking her head.

'Well Jane, what if I told you we'd found him?' The camera pushed in on Jane's bewildered face. 'He was living in Australia and took a lot of tracking down, but tonight Jane, we've flown him over to be with you.'

A surge of the sentimental music and applause.

The camera pulls back and a tanned man walks onto the set. Only the ginger hair confirms his identity. He rushes over to the sofa as Jo pulls Jane to her feet. There are tears in Brian's eyes, and Jo slips forward to address the camera and allow mother and son to embrace.

'That's all we've got time for,' Jo shouts above the noise, 'I do love a story with a happy ending, don't you? See you tomorrow.'

She winks and steps sideways to allow the camera to get right in on the embrace as the credits roll. Brian's face is tight with anguish. His mother is talking away to him, staring into a void.

'Not bad, eh,' Trevor said, reaching across to turn back to the football on the small portable they allow me to keep in the cell. 'I'm filling up.'

I could hardly speak.

'They just brushed over it all,' I managed to stutter. 'Everything. The reason why I was there. The fact that he's my half-brother.'

'Well, it's only a five-minute slot,' Trevor said.

'But don't you see, all it does is just reinforce people's prejudices, implying I was simply on the run, showing that photograph?'

'Nobody takes that much notice.'

'They never even mentioned that it was me who alerted Brian in the first place.'

'Well what...' Trevor was suddenly distracted by the television. 'Go on, go on.' He groaned as a football player sent a ball screaming over the posts into a crowd.

We were in the midst of an international football tournament, and at that moment Germany was trouncing some Middle Eastern team more interested in acrobatics than tactics. England was still in the competition, at the quarter finals stage, and the anticipation of a game against Germany and the likely outcome was at fever pitch.

Two days before, the tournament was almost cancelled when a series of bombs were located in half a dozen stadiums. A photograph arrived that day of my son James Junior, beaming in an England football strip. There was no note with it, and I imagine the historian, rather than Sally sent it.

'If my crime had been assault and battery or worse,' I said. 'I'd have been given bail. They'd never have kept me here.'

'Ah, but they think you've got it all stashed away somewhere, don't they.' Trevor's words were automatic as he followed the meandering players across the tiny screen.

'And that makes me a danger to the public does it?'

'It makes your freedom more of a liability to them. Still, I think the television people seem to know what they're doing.'

But talks had stalled with the prison authorities. They were not as keen on the idea of holding a series of crime and punishment debates here as Jo Hinchcliffe and her producer had anticipated.

The Righteous Brother, it seemed, would probably never go ahead. I was, I have to admit, disappointed. The idea had grown on me.

Reported sightings of Liz Armstrong had also become less frequent, and my lawyers had indicated that unless I was willing to shoulder some kind of responsibility without her, there would be no progress. They were of the opinion that, were I to stand trial, I would almost certainly walk free, having perhaps spent more time here than my eventual sentence would warrant.

'It's a shrinking world, Mr Turner,' Trevor said then.

'It seems that way.'

'But soon it will be your oyster again.'

'You think so,' I said.

Trevor dashed a fist at the screen, shouting in excitement, which quickly subsided.

'A shrinking world,' he repeated. 'Imagine, you can hop on a plane and be anywhere within the day. Everything's merging together, soon even the Chinese will speak English. You can communicate with somebody at the other side of the world in seconds, buy the same food as them at your corner shop. Universal brotherhood's actually becoming a reality.'

'Mind you,' he added, nodding sagely at the television, 'they should never have taken that bloody wall down.'

Thirty-three

They never stopped believing I was in on it. They thought that when the case finally stalled, as it was always in danger of doing, I would simply melt into a Swiss bank backed sunset, and they would be powerless to do anything. They were sure that Liz Armstrong, my alleged co-conspirator and - the implication was - lover, was waiting for me somewhere out there. The Med is full of them, the pencil-thin mistresses, impenetrable behind their *Gucci* shades on the balconies of five star hotels, dressed by Milanese couturiers and as still and commanding as the palms. It is also full of bullion-bedecked embezzlers in crumpled *Armani* suits, spreading their guts on yachts and traipsing brazen mayhem through overpriced bars.

They believed that it had all been a bizarre act, planned to the last meticulous detail. I would have liked to believe so myself. It isn't easy to face up to an image of yourself as a dupe and a mug, a misguided victim of too much trust, regardless of the fact that the rest of the world considers you a shrewd and impeccable actor. They even thought that those last few days, when I really got to the end of everything, were part of the act. They wouldn't for a moment accept that I could ever have been so stupid.

Legally, of course, they had the signatures to prove it. I was bound by paper chains. My name was all over everything. And as the months passed and the lawyers pressed on, the paper grew at a phenomenal rate, like some amoebic mountain that constantly doubled as an attempt was made to cleave to its centre. Money was transferred in huge sums to who knows where. It was systematically removed from insurance policies and company pension funds, all endorsed by me. I guaranteed loans which sucked up my property and whatever interests I once held in my father's businesses, and then went unpaid.

What everyone was hoping for, including those people representing me, was that I would eventually give some indication of where all that money had gone. The financial analysts had resigned themselves to never being able to trace much of it, without a little nudge in the right direction. Such had been the labyrinthine quality of its international movements. I would have been happy to oblige them, had I been able to.

Now however, it seems they won't be bothering to ask me again. Something more important has come up.

Even Trevor has stopped talking to me, gliding in with the tray solemn-faced and sniffily silent. As I feared, Jo Hinchcliffe's plans have been put on hold indefinitely. England were beaten by Germany in the semi-final.

Things that go bump in the night, first things. The moon glancing off the chimney tops.

Ronald Pickles stumbling about in my garden, colliding with the birdbath and snagging on breeze blocks, tipped off by Ansell Simmonds and on reconnaissance.

Liz Armstrong's lap-top rocking and rolling on her knees. And all those facts and figures, not allowing me to think straight.

Kevin's snout on the dash as we passed over potholes.

Sally, with James sleeping on her shoulder, throwing the door wide.

Pickles and Raven, stoned, and stubbing toes against fixtures, gleefully humping objects across the carpets.

The historian's head against the lintel. My son falling in front of me, the books cascading around us, slow-motion thuds and thumps.

Fred Flintstone's club, patted against his plastic temple, dusting the dressing table.

And then the historian's call, before there was time for it all to sink in, and Sergeant Woolin there too, reading about me in the newspaper.

Brian's mother, hair like wet rope, shrieking in my face.

My father's clarinet across the bridge of my nose.

Liz looking down at me on the staircase, hand dangling like a spider on its back.

Her expression, I realised later, had been that of my father on a number of significant occasions. It was the look I'd tried to humble in those daydreams of bringing him officially to account over his treatment of my mother. It was there too, under the Christmas tree, when Brian Bennet had received his Timex watch all those years ago.

The look was not just reserved for me, however. I saw it levelled at my mother many times, a compound of contempt, pity and disappointment.

Liz may have earned her right to become my father's successor, but I never imagined I would ever be looked at in that way again.

I tried to contemplate perfect silence, which I knew could never exist, and then I went for the spider on its back. I grabbed her wrist, there on the stairs, and the look only seemed to intensify.

And then, somehow, she wasn't there. How, I remember thinking, could she simply vanish like that, descend so quickly, with so much dignity?

I sat back down and picked up the bottle again, chewing on what she'd said. That my father would be the last to enjoy stability, and that things were different now. More vodka was needed to keep that delicious sinking sensation inside me, as if my thoughts were plunging onto a downy pillow, my body wrapped in laundered cotton sheets. But suddenly the bottle was empty, like the one containing first things.

I clambered down the stairs, and it became apparent why Liz's exit had seemed so nimble and deceptive. She'd gone over the bannister, and was lying face down on the carpet in the hall. Numbly, I turned her over. I couldn't hear her breathing, but beyond that, I had no idea if she was alive or dead. I didn't shake her, nor did I know where to feel for a pulse.

The alcohol definitely had a hold on me then, and the next thing was, I was tearing the polythene from the Christmas tree in the kitchen. Then I was draping it out next to her. I buffed all the handles and surfaces I could remember touching, and went back and retrieved the empty bottle and the letters from the stairs. These, I stuffed into her coat pockets. I was wildly stabbing around for things that might implicate me, because I had to get back to Mrs Bennet. And the one thing about driving when drunk is that mysteriously, you always get to where you want to be, even if you remember nothing about the actual journey.

Two days ago something bobbed to the surface of the lake at Walton Hall near Wakefield, an expanse of plastic glistening in the sunshine. It was fished out by the gamekeeper, who subsequently alerted the police. Forensic experts estimate the body has been in the lake for at least nine months, but as yet, can't be more certain. They have, however, already succeeded in obtaining a man's fingerprint from a bottle in the victim's coat pocket.

The search for Liz Armstrong has been called off.

Other Titles From Springboard Fiction

Miasma
by Chris Firth
ISBN: 1 901927 01 6   Price £6.95
Deserted. Lonely. Sad. Going bad. Going slowly mad. Anna Fisher
can only take so much. In this darkly humoured first novel, Chris
Firth leads us into the murky world of Anna Fisher - where
nothing is quite what it seems.

The White Room
by Karen Maitland
ISBN: 1 898311 23 4   Price £6.95
They have surveillance cameras in the White Room, watching
every move you make. In a Britain of the future where social and
cultural conflict has sharpened, Ruth is drawn into a disturbing
exploration of the forces that shape her life: her cultural identity,
her family history and a society that she no longer feels a part of.

Flood
by Tom Watts
ISBN: 1 898311 12 9   Price £4.99
Bob is back in the home town he hasn't seen for thirty years. A
remarkable first novel which moves us into an adolescent world
fraught with underlying passion and danger. A demanding,
disturbing and rewarding read.

The Labour Man
by Jim Wilson
ISBN 1 898311 01 3   Price £3.00
Can there be honour in politics? Harry Beamish, a lifelong
socialist, wrenches a marginal seat from the Tories in an election
which returns a Labour Government with a majority of one.
Unfortunate then he's done a bunk. A pre-Blair Mania novel where
the future of the Government and socialism depends on Harry.